A Happy Heart

RACHEL YODER—
Always Trouble Somewhere

Book 5

WANDA &
BRUNSTETTER

BARBOUR
PUBLISHING

Cover artist: Richard Hoit

For more information about Wanda E. Brunstetter, please access the author's Web site at the following Internet address: www.wandabrunstetter.com

Published by Barbour Publishing, Inc., P.O. Box 719, Uhrichsville, Ohio 44683, www.barbourbooks.com

Our mission is to publish and distribute inspirational products offering exceptional value and biblical encouragement to the masses.

Member of the
Evangelical Christian
Publishers Association

Printed in the United States of America.

Dedication

To the children at Riverside Christian School in Yakima, Washington. Thanks for letting me share my life as an author with you.
To Dr. Richard Ehlers and Dr. Ben Jaramillo, my kind and helpful eye doctors.

Glossary

absatz—stop
ach—oh
aldi—girlfriend
bensel—silly child
blos—bubble
boppli—baby
brieder—brothers
bruder—brother
buwe—boy
daed—dad
danki—thank you
dumm—dumb
ekelhaft—disgusting
fehlerfrie—perfect
felder—fields
fingerneggel—fingernails
gees—goat
geh—go
grank—sick
grossdaadi—grandfather
guder mariye—good morning
gut—good
hund—dog
hungerich—hungry
jah—yes
kapp—cap
kichlin—cookies
kinner—children
lachlich—laughable
lecherich—ridiculous

mamm—mom
mied—tired
mudder—mother
naas—nose
naerfich—nervous
narrish—crazy
nee—no
pescht—pest
retschbeddi—tattletale
schlang aage—snake eyes
schmaert—smart
schnell—quickly
schpassich—odd
schweschder—sister
wunderbaar—wonderful

Bass uff as du net fallscht.	Take care you don't fall.
Du kannscht mich net uffhuddle; ich bin zu schmaert	You can't confuse me; I'm too smart.
Duh net so laut schmatze.	Don't make such a noise when you eat.
Geb acht, schunscht geht's letz!	Watch out, or else things will go wrong!
Grummel net um mich rum.	Don't grumble around me.
Sei so gut.	Please.
Was in der welt?	What in all the world?
Wie geht's?	How are you?

Contents

Chapter 1

A *Lachlich* [Laughable] Day

"This is so much fun!" Ten-year-old Rachel Yoder squealed as her end of the teeter-totter shot into the air.

"My stomach feels like it's in my throat!" Audra Burkholder shouted when her side of the teeter-totter dropped down and then sprang up again.

Rachel waved one hand in the air. "Whe-e-e-e!" she hollered.

"Are you gonna ride that thing all day or does somebody else get a turn before recess is over?"

Rachel looked down. Freckle-faced Orlie Troyer stared at her. Rachel and Orlie had become friends during the year, but Rachel didn't want anyone at school to know she was friends with a boy so she kept it a secret.

"Well?" Orlie asked, tapping his foot. "Can I have a turn on the teeter-totter?"

Rachel squinted at him as her side of the teeter-totter dropped again. "Is that any way to ask for something?"

"Maybe he doesn't know how to say *sei so gut* [please]." Audra said, wrinkling her nose. "Maybe he doesn't know about manners."

Orlie squatted in the dirt, raised his hands in front of his chest and said, "Can I please have a turn on the teeter-totter?"

Rachel giggled. "You look like Jacob's dog when he sits up and begs."

Woof! Woof! Orlie bounced up and down.

"Oh, all right, you can have a turn while I get a drink of water." When Rachel climbed off the teeter-totter, she held the handle so Orlie could get on.

"This is sure fun!" Orlie shouted as his end of the teeter-totter rose. A gust of wind whipped his straw hat from his head and spun it away. He tipped his head back and howled with laughter.

Rachel raced to the pump, grabbed a paper cup, and pumped the handle up and down. When the cup was full of water she took a big drink. Then she pumped until her cup was full again.

Rachel's brother, Jacob, nudged Rachel's arm. "Save some of that for me, would ya?"

Water sloshed out of Rachel's cup and splashed her dress. "Say, watch what you're doing!"

"I figured you might need a bath." Jacob snickered.

She glared at him. "Very funny."

"I thought so, little *bensel* [silly child]." He leaned

back and laughed until his face turned red.

"Stop calling me a silly child!" Rachel dipped her finger into the cup and flicked water at Jacob's shirt. "And there's plenty of this to go around!"

"A little water doesn't bother me," Jacob said with a shrug. "In fact, it feels kind of nice on this warm spring day."

"Puh!" Rachel hurried across the playground, still holding her cup of water. "I'm back," she said as Orlie's side of the teeter-totter shot up. "It's time for you to get off now."

When the teeter-totter came down, Orlie shook his head. "I don't want to; I'm having too much fun."

"I said you could take a turn while I got a drink," Rachel announced. "So now you need to get off."

Orlie grinned but didn't budge.

Rachel glanced at Audra as Orlie's end of the teeter-totter rose and Audra's end dropped. "Can I take your place?"

Audra pushed a strand of dark hair under her *kapp* [cap] and shook her head. "Sorry, Rachel, but I'm having too much fun."

Rachel tapped her foot impatiently. If she'd known this would happen, she wouldn't have gotten off the teeter-totter. She would have waited until recess was over to get a drink.

Suddenly, Orlie leaped off the teeter-totter, sending

Audra thudding to the ground.

Audra squealed. "That wasn't nice! You should have warned me that you were getting off!"

"I decided I was thirsty!" Orlie snatched the cup out of Rachel's hand and drank. "Ah. . .that's better."

"Aren't you worried about germs?" Audra asked as she scrambled off the teeter-totter.

"Nope." Orlie took another drink and handed the cup back to Rachel.

"*Eww.*" Audra wrinkled her nose. "That's so *ekelhaft* [disgusting]!"

Rachel pushed the cup at Orlie. "You may as well keep it, 'cause I won't drink from it again."

Orlie shrugged and drank some more.

"Let's play on the swings," Rachel said to Audra.

"Okay."

The girls had only been swinging a few minutes when Orlie headed toward them, wearing his straw hat. He stopped in front of the swings, swayed back and forth, and fell on the ground. The paper cup flew out of his hand and landed in a clump of weeds. His straw hat flew off his head and landed in the dirt.

Rachel rushed over to Orlie and dropped to her knees. "Orlie's what's wrong? Are you *grank* [sick]?"

He stayed with his eyes closed, unmoving.

Audra gasped. "*Ach* [Oh], do you think he's dead?"

Rachel touched Orlie's arm, but he didn't move.

She clasped her hand over her mouth. "Maybe he *is* dead. I'd better get the teacher!"

Rachel raced for the schoolhouse, but she hadn't gone far when someone pushed her. She whirled around. There stood Orlie, wearing his tattered hat and a lopsided grin.

"Ha! Ha! I got you good!" he said, slapping his knee.

"Orlie Troyer, you should be ashamed of yourself, scaring us like that," Audra said in a shaky voice. "We thought you were a goner. *Jah* [Yes], we sure did."

Rachel shook her head. "Not me; I knew he was only pretending to be dead. I was just playing along."

Orlie's lips twitched, his shoulders shook, and he laughed so hard tears streamed down his cheeks. Then he dropped to the ground and rolled in the grass.

Orlie looked so funny that Rachel laughed, too. Soon, Audra joined in.

"Now you really do look like Jacob's dog." Rachel pointed at Orlie. "Whenever Buddy has an itch on his back he rolls in the grass just like you're doing."

Woof! Woof! Orlie sat up and begged.

Rachel giggled. "What a lachlich day!"

When Rachel and Jacob got home from school that afternoon, Rachel still felt like laughing. She'd laughed so much during recess that she couldn't concentrate on her schoolwork the rest of the day. In fact, a couple of times the words in her spelling book had looked a bit blurry. She figured it was because she had tears in her eyes from laughing so much.

"How come you're wearing such a silly grin?" Jacob asked.

"I just feel happy today."

Jacob stared at Rachel a few seconds. Finally, he shrugged and opened the door. "We're home, Mom!"

"Mmm. . .it smells like Mom's been baking today," Rachel said, heading for the kitchen. "I hope she made maple syrup cookies, because they're my favorite."

Jacob tickled Rachel in the ribs. "Every kind of cookie is your favorite, sister."

Rachel giggled and tickled Jacob back.

He snickered. "Stop that. You know how ticklish I am—especially my ribs!"

"Then you shouldn't have started it."

"What's all this silliness about?" Mom asked when they entered the kitchen.

"Rachel's in a lachlich mood today," Jacob said.

Mom removed a tray of cookies from the oven and placed them on the counter. "It's good to be in a laughable mood. When we laugh it makes us have a happy heart," she said, peering over her metal-framed glasses at Rachel.

Rachel nodded and smiled. "I've had a happy heart

most of the day."

"Wash your hands and have a seat at the table," Mom said. "Then you and Jacob can have a glass of milk and some of my freshly baked maple syrup cookies."

Rachel patted her stomach. "Yum. . .that sounds *gut* [good] to me."

Rachel and Jacob raced to the sink. They reached for the bar of soap at the same time, and—*woosh!*—it slipped off the soap dish and landed in a bowl of water sitting in the sink. *Floop!*—a spurt of water flew straight up and splashed Rachel's face.

"That soap's sure slippery." She giggled and dried her face on a towel.

"I'll bet it won't be too slippery for me." Jacob plunged his hand into the bowl of water and scooped up the soap. He'd just started to scrub his hands when the soap slipped through his fingers and landed back in the water with a splash.

Rachel chuckled. "I warned you about that, Jacob."

"Will you two please quit fooling around and wash your hands?" Mom said, shaking her head. "I'm going to see if Grandpa's up from his nap."

When Mom left the room, Jacob lunged for the soap, just as Rachel bumped his arm. The soap flew in the air, bounced onto the floor, and slid all the way to the table.

Rachel laughed as Jacob scrambled after the soap,

his feet sliding with every step he took.

Smack!—Jacob banged into the table, knocking over a carton of milk. "Oh, no," he moaned as the milk dribbled onto the floor. He took a step back, and his legs sailed out from under him. He landed on the floor with a thud.

Rachel rushed forward. "Are you all right?"

Jacob grabbed the soap and scrambled to his feet. "I'm fine—I'm not hurt a bit."

"I'd better get the mop and clean this before Mom comes back." Rachel hurried to the cleaning closet and removed the bucket and mop. She leaned the mop against the counter, set the bucket in the sink, filled it with warm water, and added some detergent.

"This bucket is sure heavy," Rachel said as she struggled to lift it out of the sink. "I'm not sure I can carry it now that it's full of water."

"Here, let me help." Jacob reached around Rachel, put the soap in the soap dish, and grabbed the bucket handle.

"Careful now. You don't want to spill any water."

"Don't worry; I know what I'm doing." Jacob lifted the bucket. *Bang!*—it bumped the edge of the sink, sloshing water all over the floor.

"Oh, no," Rachel groaned.

"Look at it this way," Jacob said with a chuckle, "the water's already out of the bucket. Now you only have to mop the floor."

Rachel grabbed the mop and pushed it back and forth. "This isn't getting the water up," she muttered. "There's too much of it on the floor."

"Say, I have an idea." Jacob tossed two dishtowels on the floor. He put his left foot on one towel and his right foot on the other; then he starting moving around the room.

"That looks like fun." Rachel grabbed two more towels, tossed them on the floor, and followed Jacob. "Whe-e-e—this *is* fun! It's almost like skating on a frozen pond!"

"*Was in der welt* [What in all the world]?"

Rachel whirled around. Mom stood inside the kitchen door with her arms folded, frowning. "Would someone please tell me what's going on in here?"

"The bar of soap fell on the floor," Rachel explained. "Then Jacob bumped the table and spilled the milk. I was going to mop up the mess, but the bucket of water spilled on the floor." Rachel drew in a quick breath. "We couldn't get the water up with the mop so we decided to use some towels."

"I'm sure you meant well, but that isn't the way to mop the floor." Mom stepped toward Rachel.

"Don't come in here!" Rachel shouted. "You might slip and fall."

"That's right," Jacob said. "You wouldn't want to

break a bone or hurt the *boppli* [baby]."

Mom placed her hands against her bulging stomach. "You're right; I do need to be careful." She pointed to the mop. "One of you needs to hold the head of the mop over the bucket and wring out the water. That will make it easier to mop."

"I'll do it!" Jacob grabbed the mop.

Mom pointed to the sopping wet towels. "Rachel, please get some clean towels to help Jacob mop up the water."

"That's what I was trying to do," Rachel said.

Mom shook her head. "Not with the towels under your feet. That's dangerous. You need to kneel on the floor, mop up the water with the dry towels, and wring them into the sink. You'll also need to wring out the wet ones you and Jacob used under your feet."

Rachel nodded. "Okay, Mom."

Mom watched until Rachel and Jacob had finished mopping up the water. When the floor was dry, she stepped into the kitchen and motioned to the table. "Shall we have cookies and milk now?"

"That sounds good to me." Jacob smacked his lips. "All that hard work made me *hungerich* [hungry]."

Mom went to the refrigerator for another carton of milk. As she placed it on the table, Grandpa entered the room. He motioned to the cookies. "I hope some of those are for me."

"Of course. Sit down and help yourself while I pour some milk," Mom said.

They all sat at the table, and Grandpa smiled at Rachel. "How was your day?"

"It's been a lachlich day." Rachel grinned at Jacob. "Isn't that right?"

He nodded.

"Laughable days are the best kind of days." Grandpa reached for a cookie and dunked it in his milk. "I learned some time ago that even if things aren't going my way it helps to put on a happy face."

"What are some things that make you feel happy?" Jacob questioned.

Grandpa wiggled his bushy gray eyebrows. "For one thing, I like to tell at least one good joke every day."

Rachel touched Grandpa's arm. "Would you tell us one now?"

"Jah, sure." Grandpa combed his fingers through the ends of his long gray beard. "Let me see now. . ."

"Why don't you tell the one about spinach?" Mom suggested. "You used to tell that joke when I was girl and it always made me laugh."

"Well, when I was a boy, my *mudder* [mother] used to say, 'Now son, eat your spinach, because it will put color in your cheeks.'" A smile spread across Grandpa's face as he leaned close to Rachel. "You know what I had to say to that?"

19

She shook her head.

Grandpa gently pinched Rachel's cheeks. "I would say to my mudder—'Who wants green cheeks?' "

Rachel giggled, Mom chuckled, and Jacob snickered.

"All's well when you laugh and grin," Grandpa said with a wink.

Rachel gave Grandpa a hug. "I'm glad you're my *grossdaadi* [grandfather]. I'm gonna try to make every day a lachlich day."

Chapter 2
Crazy Rooster

When Rachel and Jacob arrived home from school the next day, Rachel was pleased to see that Mom had set fresh fruit cups out for a snack.

Rachel's stomach rumbled as she pointed to the treats. "Mmm. . .those sure look good."

Mom smiled. "Wash your hands and take a seat at the table."

Jacob raced for the kitchen sink, but Rachel hurried to the bathroom. After the trouble she'd had yesterday with the soap and water, she wasn't about to wash her hands at the same sink with Jacob.

When Rachel returned to the kitchen, Jacob was already eating his fruit and drinking a glass of milk. "*Danki* [Thank you], Mom, for fixing us such a nice snack," Rachel said.

"Jah, danki." Jacob smacked his lips, chomped on a hunk of apple, and slurped his milk.

"*Duh net so laut schmatze* [Don't make such a noise

when you eat]," Mom said. "Eat a little quieter." She pulled out a chair and sat beside Rachel. "How was school today?"

"It was good." Rachel plucked a piece of banana from her fruit cup and popped it in her mouth. "Audra and I played on the teeter-totter during recess again. It was lots of fun."

Mom smiled. "It's nice that you and Audra have become such good friends."

Rachel nodded. When Audra had first moved to Lancaster County, she and Rachel hadn't gotten along so well. That was mainly because Rachel had missed her cousin Mary, who'd moved to Indiana. After Rachel realized that Audra was nice and also needed a friend, she and Audra had gotten along quite well.

"Where's Grandpa this afternoon? Is he taking a nap?" Rachel asked.

Mom shook her head. "He and your *daed* [dad] went to town to pick up some supplies for the new greenhouse they hope to build."

"Did Henry go with them?" Jacob asked.

"No, he went to see his *aldi* [girlfriend], Nancy."

Rachel frowned. "I'm disappointed that Grandpa went to town without me. He said I could help him choose some of the plants for the greenhouse."

"I don't think he and your daed are looking for flowers today," Mom said. "I believe they went to get lumber and supplies to build the greenhouse."

Rachel smiled. She felt better knowing Grandpa hadn't left her out of his greenhouse plans. Maybe they could shop for flowers and plants soon.

"When you two are finished with your snack, I have a few chores for you to do," Mom said.

Jacob's forehead wrinkled. "What chores?"

"I'd like you to clean the horses' stalls while Rachel feeds and waters the chickens and checks for eggs." Mom peered at Rachel over the top of her glasses. "I was going to do that earlier, but I went over to Anna Miller's for a visit after you left for school. I stayed longer than I'd planned, so I didn't get to the chicken coop."

Rachel didn't look forward to taking care of the chickens, but she knew better than to argue with Mom. "Can we play after we finish our chores?" she asked.

"Of course." Mom patted Rachel's arm. "The sooner you get the jobs done, the sooner you can play."

Jacob put an orange slice between his lips and bit. A squirt of juice hit Rachel's forehead.

"Hey! Watch what you're doing!" Rachel dashed to the sink, splashed cold water on her face, and patted it dry with a clean towel. "I'll bet you did that on purpose," she said when she returned to the table.

"Did not."

"Did so."

"Did not."

"Did—"

Mom clapped her hands. "If you don't stop squabbling you may not play when you're done with your chores."

"Sorry," Rachel and Jacob both mumbled.

Grinning, Jacob looked over at Rachel and said, "I love you, *schweschder* [sister]."

On her way to the chicken coop, Rachel spotted Buddy sleeping on the roof of his doghouse. His nose was tucked between his paws, and his floppy ears covered both eyes. Rachel hadn't liked Buddy when he'd first come to live with them, because she was afraid he would hurt her cat. But Buddy and Cuddles had become friends, just like Rachel and Audra. Now Rachel only had to worry about Buddy giving her sloppy wet kisses. She tried to stay away from Buddy whenever Jacob let him out of his dog run.

Rachel glanced at the barn, where Jacob was cleaning the horses' stalls. A gray and white ball of fur streaked across the lawn and ducked into the barn. Rachel figured Cuddles was probably after a mouse.

Rachel opened the door to the chicken coop. As soon as she stepped inside she knew she was in for trouble. *Squawk! Squawk! Squawk!* Hector, the biggest, noisiest rooster, flapped his wings and flew around the coop, dropping feathers everywhere.

Rachel didn't know if Hector was carrying on because he was hungry, or if he was just being ornery. As long as he didn't try to peck Rachel or get in her way, she didn't care how crazy he acted.

Rachel opened the lid on the bucket of chicken feed, scooped some out, and poured it into the feeders. Squawking and flapping their wings, all the chickens in the coop swarmed around the feeders, pecking at the food.

While the chickens ate, Rachel took the water dishes outside. Using the hose, she filled them with fresh water and hauled them back to the coop. She'd just set the last one inside when Hector started carrying on again.

Squawk! Squawk! Cock-a-doodle-do! He strutted across the floor with his wings outstretched. When he reached the open door, he flew past Rachel and landed in the yard. With another noisy squawk, Hector headed straight for Buddy's dog run. He stuck his head through a hole in the fence and grabbed food from Buddy's dish.

Rachel dashed across the yard, waving her hands. "Stop that, you *narrish* [crazy] rooster! You have your own food in the coop!"

Hector kept eating. *Chomp! Chomp! Chomp!*

Rachel clapped her hands. "Buddy, wake up! Hector's stealing your food!"

Buddy opened his eyes, stretched, and scratched his ear.

Rachel pointed to the rooster. "Don't you care that he's robbing your food? Chase him away, Buddy!"

With a shake of his furry head, Buddy jumped to his feet and leaped off the doghouse. *Woof! Woof! Woof!* He rammed the fence with his nose.

Hector screeched and jerked away from Buddy's dish, but when he tried to pull his head through the hole in the fence he got stuck. *Bawk! Bawk! Bawk!*

Grrr. Woof! Woof! Buddy swiped at the rooster's head with his paw.

Bawk! Bawk!

Woof! Woof! Woof!

"What's all the ruckus about?" Jacob shouted as he raced from the barn. "What's wrong with Buddy?"

Rachel pointed to the chicken. "Hector was trying to steal Buddy's food. Then Buddy went after him, and now Hector's head is stuck. Can you do something, Jacob? I'm afraid Buddy might hurt him."

Even though Rachel had wanted Hector to stop eating Buddy's food, she didn't want Buddy to hurt the poor critter.

"Jah, okay. I'll see what I can do." Jacob opened the gate to Buddy's dog run and stepped inside. "Here, Buddy. Come, boy!"

Grrr. Buddy was nose to beak with the rooster and wouldn't budge.

"Bad dog! Come when I call!" Jacob grabbed Buddy's collar and pulled him away from the chicken. "See if you can get the rooster's head out now," he said to Rachel.

Rachel squatted beside Hector and placed her hands around his neck. Slowly, gently, she pulled.

Bawk! Bawk! Hector's head popped free. Looking a bit dazed, he stood there a few seconds, shook his head, and then wobbled across the yard, crowing all the way. *Cock-a-doodle-do!*

"What a narrish chicken," Rachel muttered. "He ought to know better than to stick his beak where it doesn't belong."

Jacob snickered. "Jah, just like some people I know."

Rachel glared at him. "What's that supposed to mean?"

"Oh, nothing." Jacob patted the dog's head, stepped out of the dog run, and closed the gate. "Be good, Buddy. I'll come back to play with you after I finish my chores in the barn."

Buddy plodded back to his dog house; only this time he crawled inside instead of jumping on top.

"That was a close call for the rooster," Rachel said as she walked beside Jacob.

Jacob shrugged. "That's what the critter gets for trying to steal Buddy's food."

Rachel's brows furrowed. "How would you like it if some big animal came along and tried to eat Buddy?"

"I wouldn't like it," he said.

"When the rooster was acting crazy inside the chicken coop I was angry with him, and when he went after Buddy's food, it really made me mad." Rachel sighed. "Even so, I didn't want the chicken to get hurt."

"I see what you mean. I'll have to think about what I'm saying from now on."

"Does that mean you won't tease me anymore?"

"I'm your *bruder* [brother], so I'll probably still tease," Jacob said. "But I'd never do anything on purpose to hurt you."

Rachel smiled and headed for the chicken coop. It was comforting to know Jacob would never hurt her intentionally. She just hoped he would stop teasing her.

"Where are you going?" Jacob called. "Haven't you finished feeding the chickens?"

"Jah, but I forgot to check for eggs."

"I have one more stall to clean, and then I'll take Buddy for a walk." Jacob disappeared into the barn.

Rachel stepped into the coop and picked up the basket Mom kept near the door. Checking under each hen, she found only three eggs. "Guess that's better than none," she said, heading back to the house.

When Rachel entered the kitchen, she was surprised

that it was empty. She had figured Mom would have started supper by now. She cleaned the eggs and put them in the refrigerator, then headed to the living room to get the book she'd left there last night.

Rachel found Mom asleep on the sofa, so she picked up the book and tiptoed quietly out of the room.

Outside, Rachel sat on the porch swing and opened the book. She'd only read a few pages when she heard a horrible shriek, followed by—*thump-thump-thump!*

"I hope Buddy isn't after Cuddles now," Rachel moaned. She set the book on the swing and stepped into the yard to investigate.

She scanned the area, but didn't see anything un-usual.

Thumpety-thump-thump!

Rachel bent down and peered under the porch. Two beady eyes stared back at her.

Hector wobbled out from under the porch, shaking his head and ruffling his feathers.

Rachel's mouth fell open. The crazy rooster had a yogurt cup stuck on his beak!

"Hold still, Hector." Rachel crept closer to the chicken. "Let me get that off you."

Squawk! Squawk! The rooster hopped onto the porch, shaking his head and flapping his wings.

Rachel felt sorry for the bird, although she still

laughed. The critter looked hilarious, dancing around the porch, flipping his head from side to side.

She tried to corner Hector between the swing and the porch railing, but he darted around her and leaped off the porch, leaving red feathers in her hands.

Rachel ran into the yard after the rooster, but every time she came close, he turned another way. With a frustrated sigh, she went to get Jacob.

"Are you done cleaning the horses' stalls?" she asked when she found Jacob sitting on a bale of straw.

He nodded.

"I need your help again."

"What is it this time, Rachel?"

"Hector got his beak stuck in a yogurt cup, and I can't catch him to get it off."

"No problem. I'll capture that crazy rooster."

Rachel followed Jacob out of the barn. They found Hector banging the yogurt cup against the horses' watering trough.

"I'll catch him!" Jacob dashed across the yard, took a flying leap, and landed in the water trough with a splash!

Rachel laughed so hard she could barely breathe, and tears rolled down her cheeks.

"That wasn't funny," Jacob mumbled as he pulled himself out of the trough. He shook his head, splattering water all over Rachel.

Rachel jumped back. "Hey! Watch what you're doing!"

"Since you thought it was so funny to see me wet, I thought I'd share the water with you."

Rachel was about to tell Jacob what she thought, when the rooster wobbled up and stopped at her feet. He tipped his head back and looked at her as if to say, "Would you please get this thing off my beak?"

Rachel grasped the cup with both hands, and— *floop!*—it popped right off!

Hector shook his head and flew up to the fence. Tilting his head back, he let out a garbled, *Cocker-doodle-de-do!*

Rachel looked at Jacob, and they both laughed. "I'm glad we live on a farm," she said. "Around here something funny is always going on."

Chapter 3

Disappointments

On Saturday morning a few weeks later, Rachel headed down the driveway to the mailbox. The harsh wind smacked against her body with such force she nearly toppled over. The ties on her kapp whipped around her face. The spring day had started so nicely. She hoped the wind would die down soon so she could do something fun. Maybe later she could jump on the trampoline, play in the barn with Cuddles, or catch some frogs at the creek. Those were always fun things to do.

Rachel opened the mailbox and pulled out a stack of mail. "All right! I got a letter from Mary!" she exclaimed when she saw the envelope on top addressed to her.

Rachel raced up the driveway, eager to read her cousin's words. She sat on the porch step and ripped open the letter. She'd only read the first two words, when—*whoosh!*—a gust of wind tore the letter from her hands, carrying it across the yard, along with some blowing loose straw from the piles stacked near the barn.

Rachel placed the rest of the mail on the small table near the back door and raced after the runaway letter. It zoomed across the grass, flew into the maple tree, and fluttered to the ground.

Rachel lunged for it, and—*whoosh!*—another gust of wind carried the letter away.

"Come back here!" Rachel shouted as she continued the chase. No way was she going to let Mary's letter get away from her!

Huffing and puffing, she dashed after the letter, but it drifted on the wind and whooshed away again. She watched it sail through the air and land in the pasture where Pap's herd of brown and white cows grazed.

The wind settled down and Rachel climbed over the fence. Her fingers almost touched the letter, when—*snort!*—one of the cows nudged the letter with its nose, and the piece of paper flew against the fence and stuck.

"Ah-ha! I've got you now!" Rachel grabbed the letter, and, *rip!*—it tore right in two!

"Oh, no," she groaned. "How can I read Mary's letter now?"

Rachel raced back to the porch, scooped up the mail on the table, and opened the door. "The mail's here," she said when she entered the kitchen.

Mom motioned to the table. "Just put it over there."

"I got a letter from Mary, but the wind took it away. Then one of Pap's cows nudged it with its nose and it stuck to the fence. When I grabbed the paper, it ripped in two!" Rachel frowned and lifted both halves of the letter.

Mom set the broom aside. "Lay the pieces on the table and we'll tape them together." She got clear tape from the desk, taped the pieces, and handed the letter to Rachel. "Here you go. . .good as new."

Rachel sat at the table to read Mary's letter. *"Dear Rachel: How are you—"* She squinted as she tried to figure out the next words. They looked blurry. "I wonder why Mary wrote with such tiny letters," she mumbled. "I can't read some of the words."

"Maybe you're having problems reading the letter because it was torn. Would you like me to see if I can read it?" Mom asked.

Rachel nodded and handed her the letter.

Mom pushed her glasses to the bridge of her nose and began to read. *"Dear Rachel: How are you doing? Are you having nice weather there in Pennsylvania? It's nice here in Indiana, and I'm glad it's spring. Last Saturday our family went to the Fun Spot amusement park. We liked it so much! We went on lots of rides and saw some interesting animals. I wish you could have been with us."*

"I wish we could go someplace like that," Rachel interrupted. "All we ever do is stay around here and work."

"That's not true," Mom said. "We've had some fun times with Esther and Rudy whenever they've come here for supper or we've gone over to their house."

Rachel bit her bottom lip. Visiting her big sister was nice, but it wasn't as much fun as going to an amusement park. Maybe she should ask Pap to take them to Hershey Park. She'd heard a lot of fun rides were there.

"Where's Pap?" she asked.

"He's in the barn."

Rachel jumped up and started for the door.

"Where are you going?" Mom called.

"I need to talk to Pap."

"What about Mary's letter? Don't you want to hear what else she said?"

Rachel nodded. "Jah, okay. I guess I can talk to Pap after you're done."

Mom smiled and continued to read. *"How's Cuddles doing? My cat, Stripes, is fine, but I think he misses her. Maybe when we come for a visit, we can bring Stripes."*

"Does she say when that might be?" Rachel asked.

Mom shook her head. "I'm sure it won't be until after school gets out."

"What else does Mary say?"

"Let's see. . ." Mom's glasses had slipped to the end of her nose, and she pushed them back in place again. *"I went to my friend Betty's house yesterday afternoon. We baked chocolate chip cookies and drew some pictures. We both like horses, so that's what we drew. Next week Betty's coming over to my house with her mamm* [mom], *and we're going to bake some pies."*

Rachel smiled. At one time she would have been jealous to hear what Mary had done with her new friend. Now that Rachel had Audra as a friend, she didn't mind so much when Mary mentioned Betty in her letters.

"Is there more?" she asked Mom.

"Just a bit," Mom said. "Here's how Mary closes her letter: *'Take care and write back soon. I'm looking forward to seeing you again. Love, Mary.'"*

"Danki for reading the letter to me." Rachel raced for the back door. "I'm going to the barn to see Pap," she called over her shoulder.

Rachel found Pap, Jacob, and Henry grooming the horses. "Can I speak to you a minute?" she asked Pap.

He nodded. "Jah, sure, what did you want to say?"

"I got a letter from Mary today." Rachel gulped in a quick breath. "She said her folks took her to an amusement park in Indiana."

"That's nice." Pap brushed old Tom's back.

"She said they had fun and went on lots of rides and saw some animals."

"Umm. . .I see."

Rachel moved closer to old Tom and rubbed his soft nose. "Could we hire a driver to take us to Hershey Park some Saturday? I think it would be fun to go on some of the rides there." She looked up at Pap. "Can we go? Can we go there soon?"

Pap shook his head. "You know I'm in the middle of spring planting. We'll have too much farm work for several months. Besides, your mamm isn't feeling up to such an outing right now."

"Maybe after the baby is born—then can we go to Hershey Park?"

"I don't know, Rachel. We'll have to wait and see."

"Couldn't we go sometime this summer, before school starts again?" Rachel persisted.

"If we go at all, it probably won't be this year," Pap said as he combed old Tom's mane. "Since the boppli will be born in July, he or she will be too young to make a trip like that."

"Then when can we go?"

"I don't know, Rachel. We'll have to see."

"I never get to do anything fun," Rachel mumbled as she left the barn. She was halfway to the house when she saw Grandpa heading her way.

"I'm going to town to pick up some supplies for your daed." Grandpa smiled. "Would you like to go along, Rachel?"

She nodded eagerly. "Jah, Grandpa. That sounds like fun. Will you look for plants for the greenhouse, too?"

"Not today. Your daed's real busy with farm chores right now. He won't start on my greenhouse until late May or early June."

"But June's two months away."

"I know." Grandpa smiled and patted Rachel's head. "We must learn to be patient. Good things come to those who wait, you know."

Rachel nodded, trying not to show disappointment. She looked forward to helping in Grandpa's greenhouse, but she wished they didn't have to wait so long.

"Do you still want to ride to town with me?" Grandpa asked.

"Oh, jah. It will give us a chance to visit awhile."

"Okay, but you'd better go inside and check with your mamm first," Grandpa said. "While you're doing that, I'll get the horse and buggy ready to go."

Rachel hugged Grandpa and sprinted to the house. She found Mom sitting in front of her sewing machine. "Grandpa's going to town and he invited me to go along. Is that okay with you?"

"Not today, Rachel," Mom said as she pumped her feet up and down on the treadle to get the machine going.

"If I can't ride to town with Grandpa, can I go to Audra's and play?"

"Sorry, but no."

"How come?"

"Because you—"

"Can I go outside and jump on the trampoline?"

Mom shook her head. "If you hadn't interrupted, I was going to say you may not play until all your chores are done."

"But I finished my chores after breakfast."

"You finished the ones you normally do, but as soon as I finish mending these trousers for Jacob, I want to do some cleaning." Mom looked up and smiled at Rachel. "I'll need your help."

Rachel bit the end of a fingernail. She'd done enough work today. It wasn't fair that Mom expected her to do more. She felt like all she ever did was work.

"Don't bite your *fingerneggel* [fingernails], Rachel," Mom said. "I've told you it's a bad habit. Besides, your fingernails are full of germs."

"Sorry," Rachel mumbled. "I wish I didn't have more chores to do. I was hoping to do something fun today."

"After we finish the cleaning, maybe we can walk

to the creek. That sounds like fun, doesn't it?" Mom asked.

Rachel shrugged. If she went to the creek she could probably wade in the water and look for frogs, but it wouldn't be nearly as much fun as going to town with Grandpa.

Mom pushed away from the sewing machine. "I'm done with my mending now, so while I clean the living room floor and dust, I'd like you to wash the living room windows."

Rachel groaned. Washing windows didn't sound like fun at all!

She'd just entered the utility room to get the window cleaning solution and a clean rag when she heard the back door creak open, and Grandpa called, "Rachel, are you ready to go to town? I have the horse and buggy ready to go!"

Rachel stepped out of the utility room and met him with a scowl. "I can't go to town with you, Grandpa. Mom says I have to do some cleaning." Her chin quivered and she blinked a couple of times to keep her tears from spilling over.

Grandpa pulled Rachel to his side and hugged her. "It's okay. You can go to town with me another time when you're not so busy."

"I'll probably always be busy," she said with a groan. "The older I get, the more chores I have to do."

Grandpa patted the top of her head. "Then make your chores fun."

"How do I do that?"

"Make a game out of what you're doing."

Rachel tilted her head. "Huh?"

"Let me give you an example," Grandpa said. "When I was a *buwe* [boy] and had to wash dishes, I pretended that the dishes were *kinner* [children], swimming in a pond." A smile stretched across Grandpa's face. "It was fun to make the dishes dive into the pond. It made lots of bubbles, and they splashed in my face."

Rachel giggled as she pictured Grandpa dropping silverware into the soapy water and bubbles breaking on his nose. "Guess I'll have to try that the next time I do the dishes."

"It doesn't just have to be when you're doing the dishes," Grandpa said. "You can pretend all sorts of things while you're doing different chores."

Rachel nodded. "I'll try that on the chores I do today."

Grandpa hugged her again. "Good girl." He turned toward the door. "Well, I'd best be on my way. I'll see you later this afternoon."

Rachel hurried to the living room. She figured if she got the windows cleaned quickly, Mom might let her play.

She held the spray bottle up to the window. *Squirt! Squirt!* She squeezed the lever until the window had plenty of liquid. *Swish! Swish! Swish!* She pretended she was painting a pretty picture as she swiped the rag up, down, and all over the window.

"How's it going?" Mom asked, stepping up to Rachel.

"Fine. I'm almost done with my picture."

Mom eyebrows lifted as she looked at Rachel. "What picture?"

Rachel's cheeks warmed. "Oh, I—uh—pretended I was painting a picture while I washed the window."

"I see." Mom peered at the window. "Ach, Rachel, look at all the streaks you've left! You'll have to do that window again."

Rachel leaned close to the glass and squinted. "I don't see any streaks."

"Right there." Mom pointed to a spot on the lower half of the window. "Do you see it now?"

Rachel nodded. She saw it, but it looked fuzzy. "Something must be wrong with the window cleaner," she said.

"Here, let me try." Mom took the rag and bottle from Rachel. *Squirt! Squirt! Swish! Swish! Swish!* "There, that's better. You probably weren't rubbing hard enough." She handed the window cleaner and rag back to Rachel.

Rachel leaned close to the window again and

looked outside. "I think you must have missed a few spots, because some things in the yard look blurry."

Squirt! Squirt! Swish. . .swish. . .swish—she scrubbed at the window some more.

"You can stop now, Rachel. That window's as clean as it can be."

Rachel leaned close to the window again and stared outside. Everything still looked blurry, but if Mom thought the window was clean enough, she wouldn't say anything more. "Now can I go outside and play?" Rachel asked hopefully.

Mom shook her head. "We still have more cleaning to do."

"Like what?"

"I'd like you to shake the living room rugs while I mop the kitchen floor."

"Is that all you need me to do?"

Mom's glasses had slipped to the end or her nose, and she pushed them back in place. "I believe so; unless I think of something else." She smiled and left the room.

Rachel bent down and grabbed the small braided rug in front of the sofa. She hauled it to the porch. Pretending the porch was a trampoline and she was jumping on it, she gave the rug a few good shakes. Then she draped it over the railing. She went back to the living room to get the rug in front of Grandpa's rocking chair. She gave that a couple of shakes, imagining again that she was bouncing up and down on the trampoline. When her arms grew tired, she draped the rug over the railing, and returned to get another rug near the front door.

When Rachel stepped onto the porch again, she gasped. Buddy had one of the rugs in his mouth! *Grr.* He growled and shook it for all he was worth!

"*Absatz* [Stop]! You're a bad *hund* [dog]!" Rachel tugged on the dog's collar, but he didn't let go of the rug.

*Grr. . .Grr. . .*Buddy continued to shake and growl.

Rachel gritted her teeth and tugged Buddy's collar again. "If you tear a hole in that rug you'll be in big trouble with Mom!" She thought about the towel Buddy had stolen from the laundry basket and ripped in two. Mom hadn't been happy about that at all!

Grr. . .Grr. . .Shake! Shake! Shake!

Rachel let go of Buddy's collar and cupped her hands around her mouth. "Jacob Yoder, you'd better come get your dog, *schnell* [quickly]!"

No response.

Rachel figured Jacob must still be in the barn helping Pap and Henry groom the horses. She thought about going to get him but was afraid if she left, Buddy would tear the rug.

Suddenly, an idea popped into Rachel's head. She ran down the porch steps, raced to the water spigot, and turned on the hose. Aiming it at the porch, she sprayed Buddy's face.

Buddy let go of the rug and howled. He leaped off the porch, circled around Rachel, jumped up, and— *slurp!*—licked her face.

"Yuk! Get down, you big hairy mutt!" Rachel shot Buddy with another spray of water.

Woof! Woof! Woof! Buddy circled her again, bounded onto the porch, and darted into the house.

"Oh, great! I should have shut the door!"

Rachel raced into the house. When she heard Mom scream, "Ach, no!" she knew Buddy must be in the kitchen. She ran after him.

"Look what this dog has done!" Mom clucked her tongue as she pointed to the muddy paw prints on the kitchen floor. "Now I'll have to wash the floor again!"

"I'm sorry, Mom," Rachel panted, "but that flea-bitten hund grabbed one of the rugs and wouldn't let go. He kept growling and shaking the rug." She gulped in a quick breath of air. "So I turned on the hose and sprayed him with water. He let go, but then he ran around the yard, got his feet dirty, and ran into the house before I could stop him."

Buddy circled Mom, barking and chasing his tail. *Woof! Woof! Woof!*

When he made the next pass, Mom bent down and grabbed his collar. "Rachel, take this hund outside and put him in his dog run! Then hang the rug on the clothesline, because I'm sure it got wet from the hose."

"Okay, Mom," Rachel said as she led Buddy out the back door.

Woof! Woof! Woof! Buddy's tail swished the skirt of Rachel's dress.

"You're nothing but trouble," she muttered.

By the time Rachel had put Buddy in his dog run and hung the rug on the line to dry, she was tired. She trudged up the porch steps, wondering what other chores Mom had for her to do. At this rate, they would never get to take that walk, and she would probably have no time for play.

When Rachel entered the house, she peeked into the kitchen. The floor was clean, but Mom was no longer there. Thinking Mom might have gone to the living room to do more cleaning, Rachel headed in that direction. She found Mom lying on the sofa with her eyes shut.

Rachel tiptoed across the room. "Are you sleeping?" she whispered.

Mom opened her eyes. "Almost."

"What about our walk to the creek?"

Mom released a noisy yawn. "I'd better not today, Rachel. After all that cleaning, I'm really tired. You're free to go outside and play while I take a nap."

Rachel shook her head. "I'm not in the mood now." She trudged up the stairs, stomped into her room, and fell on the bed. "Always trouble somewhere!"

She stretched her arms over her head until they bumped the headboard. "We can't go to Hershey Park; I couldn't go to town with Grandpa; the greenhouse won't be built until June; I had to do chores all afternoon; and now Mom's too tired to walk to the creek. What a disappointing day!"

Chapter 4

Seeing Is Believing

"Did ya see that pretty butterfly?" Orlie asked Rachel when she and Jacob entered the schoolyard Monday morning.

Rachel looked around. "Where? I don't see a butterfly."

"Over there!" Orlie pointed to a bush across the yard. "Do you see it?"

Rachel grunted. "No, I don't. Are you teasing me, Orlie?"

"Of course not." Orlie's nose twitched when he gave her a crooked grin. "I never tease, you know that."

"Jah, right! You tease a lot, and I'm sure you're teasing about the butterfly."

"No, I'm not." Orlie poked Rachel's arm. "Maybe you can't see the butterfly because your eyes have gone bad. Maybe you should go to the doctor and get your eyes checked."

"I don't need a doctor. I can see just fine!" Rachel's

long skirt swished around her legs as she ran through the grass. She was almost to the schoolhouse steps when she heard a squeal. She looked around. She saw Audra cowering in the bushes near the porch.

"What's wrong?" Rachel asked.

Audra's chin trembled. "I—I dropped my backpack." She stood up and pointed to the backpack, lying in the bushes. "I—I'm afraid to pick it up b-because there's a spider on it."

Rachel knew Audra was afraid of bugs, but she'd never realized how much until now. The poor girl was actually shivering, and it wasn't the least bit cold.

Rachel stared at Audra's backpack. "I don't see a spider. It must have crawled away."

Audra continued to point. "It's still there. See. . .on the flap."

Rachel squinted. "I don't see a spider. Are you teasing me, Audra?"

"Of course not. Why would I tease about seeing a spider?" Audra's face turned red. "Would you kill it for me, Rachel?"

Rachel shook her head. "Huh-uh. If there is a spider on your backpack, then the little critter has the right to live." She turned toward the porch.

Audra dashed to Rachel and clutched her arm. "Please, don't go. I—I need you to kill that spider!"

"Du kannscht mich net uffhuddle; ich bin zu schmaert

[You can't confuse me; I'm too smart]," Rachel said.

"I'm not trying to confuse you. There really is a spider," Audra said in a shaky voice.

Rachel grunted. "If you think so, you'd better kill it yourself, because I'm not going to."

"*Eww*. . .I could never do that! What if it jumped at me?" Audra thrust out her lower lip. "Please, Rachel. If you won't kill the spider, will you at least get it off my backpack?"

With a frustrated grunt, Rachel bent, scooped up the backpack, and gave it a shake. "Is the spider gone now?"

Audra studied the backpack and nodded. "Jah, it's gone. Danki, Rachel."

Rachel plodded up the stairs, shaking her head. She couldn't believe Audra was afraid of a little bitty spider. She couldn't believe she hadn't been able to see it on Audra's backpack, either.

What was going on? First the butterfly Orlie said was there but Rachel never saw, and now an invisible spider! Either she was going blind, or Orlie and Audra were in cahoots and had decided to make this "tease Rachel day."

Well, if anyone else saw anything that wasn't really there, Rachel would just play along. No point giving them the satisfaction of thinking they'd pulled a fast one on her!

When the teacher, Elizabeth, dismissed the scholars

for recess that morning, Rachel headed straight for the swings. She was the first one there, so she got to choose her favorite swing.

She started by making the swing go side to side, then she swirled around a couple of times until she felt dizzy. Finally—*pump. . .pump. . .push. Pump. . .pump. . .push*—she moved her legs fast, and was soon swinging so high she felt like a bird soaring up to the sky. "Whee. . .this is so much fun!"

"Did you see that pretty bird in the tree over there?" Orlie asked when he joined Rachel on the swings.

"What bird?"

"That one—in the maple tree."

Rachel slowed her swing so she could get a better look. She did see the bird, but it looked like a blurry blob.

"Do you see it, Rachel?" Orlie asked.

"Uh—jah, it's real pretty."

Orlie started pumping his legs really fast. "Bet I can swing higher than you can."

"Bet you can't." *Pump. . .pump. . .push. Pump. . .pump. . .push*. Rachel got her swing going as high as she could.

"You'd better watch out, or you'll fly right off and land in the tree with that bird!" Orlie hollered.

Rachel giggled as she flew up. "My swing's higher

than yours," she shouted. "I win!"

"You didn't give me a fair chance. I can go higher if I want to."

"No you can't, because recess is over." Rachel started to drag her feet to slow the swing. "See, all the scholars are heading inside."

Orlie groaned. "I'll beat you the next time; just wait and see."

"That's what you think, Orlie Troyer!" Rachel jumped off the swing, dashed across the yard, and— *floop*—dropped to her knees!

"What happened?" Audra rushed to Rachel and helped her to her feet.

Rachel brushed the dirt from her dress. "I—I guess I must have tripped on something."

"I think it was that." Audra motioned to the hose stretched across the yard. "Didn't you see it?"

Rachel shook her head. "I—I wasn't looking down."

"Are you hurt?"

Rachel inspected her knees. "I'm okay. My knees aren't even bleeding."

"You need to be more careful." Audra patted Rachel's back. "Were you in a hurry to get inside?"

"Jah, I was." Rachel started moving toward the schoolhouse again. She was almost to the porch when she heard a bird twittering from the tree nearby. She tipped her head back and squinted. There was that blurry blob again. She didn't understand why every-thing looked so fuzzy lately. Could something be wrong with her eyes? Would she need to see a doctor? Oh, she hoped not!

"Are you gonna play ball with us?" Jacob asked Rachel during lunch recess that day.

Rachel shrugged. "I thought I might swing or play on the teeter-totter with Audra."

"Aw, come on, Rachel." Jacob nudged her arm. "You're a good ball player; we need you."

"I'd rather not."

"Please, Rachel. I'd like you to be on my team."

"Oh, okay," Rachel finally agreed. She was pleased that Jacob thought she was good at playing ball. He didn't often say nice things to her.

Rachel followed Jacob to the baseball field. "Play center field," he said.

"Why can't I play second or first base?"

"You're good at catching fly balls, so that's where I want you to go."

"Where are you gonna play?" she asked.

"I'll be the pitcher." Jacob cupped his hands around his mouth. "Orlie, you're on my team, too, so play in left field."

"Let's get the other team out, schnell," Orlie said to Rachel. "I can't wait 'til I'm up to bat, because I plan to bat a homerun!"

"You always like to win," Rachel mumbled as she walked to center field.

"What was that?" Orlie called.

"Oh, nothing."

The first few balls never made it past the infield, so that made two outs. Then came a couple of foul balls. Rachel wondered if any balls would ever come her way, when suddenly—*smack!*—Aaron King hit a ball that sailed right over Jacob's head.

"Catch it, Rachel!" Orlie hollered. "Get that ball!"

Rachel saw a blur of white whiz past her head, but when she reached out to grab it, the ball flew over her glove. She lunged for it and fell on her face. *Oomph!*

"Are you all right, Rachel?" Audra called from first base. "Your *naas* [nose] isn't bleeding, I hope."

Rachel touched her nose and was relieved not to see any blood on her fingers. Last month, when she'd been playing ball, she'd gotten smacked in the nose and ended up with a nasty nosebleed.

"What's the matter with you, Rachel?" Jacob called. "Didn't you see that ball coming?"

"I saw it. I just missed, that's all." Rachel wasn't about to admit that the ball had looked like a blurry snowball whizzing past her head.

Jacob frowned. "Jah, well, you'd better keep a close watch on the ball from now on."

Rachel wrinkled her nose. "Maybe I should have

played on the teeter-totter or swings. At least no one would be picking on me."

"Oh, don't be like that," Jacob said. "When our team's up to bat I'm sure you'll do better."

Maybe Jacob's right, Rachel thought. *I am pretty good at hitting the ball. I might even make a homerun. That would show Orlie.*

Rachel sat on the bench waiting for her turn to bat. Orlie went first and hit a ball that took him to second base. Then Jacob was up, and his ball sailed into right field and brought Orlie home. Lonnie Byler was up next, but he struck out. Then Audra batted, and she struck out, too.

Now it was Rachel's turn. She stepped up to the plate, took her stance, and waited for the ball. It came quickly—*swish!* Rachel swung—and missed.

"Strike one!" David Miller shouted.

"Don't swing unless it's right over the plate," Jacob called to Rachel.

"I won't!"

The pitcher threw the ball again, but the blur of white whizzed right past Rachel.

"Strike two!"

Rachel gripped the bat tighter. The fuzzy white ball came again—*swish!* She swung hard—and missed.

"Strike three—you're out!"

Rachel groaned. So much for getting a homerun!

So much for showing Orlie how well she could play! He probably thought she was a real loser today.

"What's the matter with you, Rachel?" Jacob grumbled. "You acted like you couldn't even see that ball!"

"I could see it. I just missed, that's all."

Jacob wrinkled his nose. "Jah, well, I'll think twice before I ask you to be on my team again."

"That's fine with me. I'd rather play on the swings anyway!" Rachel dropped the bat and hurried away. She'd never admit it to Jacob, but she was worried. Was it possible that she hadn't seen the ball clearly because something was wrong with her eyes? Oh, she hoped not!

Chapter 5

Blurry Words

"Are you coming with me to see Grandpa and Grandma Yoder?" Rachel asked Jacob as they walked home from school the next day.

"I don't think so," Jacob said. "Pap's gonna need my help this afternoon."

"When I saw Grandma at church the other day, she said Grandpa was going fishing today, and she thought it would be nice if she and I baked something." Rachel smiled. "I'll probably bring home some cookies."

"Just be sure you don't mess up the recipe like you did before."

Rachel glared at Jacob. "Why do you always say mean things?"

"I was just stating facts."

Rachel kicked a stone and kept walking. She figured if she said anything back to Jacob they'd end up arguing, and she didn't want to arrive at Grandma's in a bad mood. That would ruin their afternoon together.

"Goodbye," Jacob said as they approached the driveway leading to Grandma and Grandpa Yoder's house. "I'll see you at supper."

Rachel turned up the driveway, calling over her shoulder, "Have fun in the *felder* [fields]!"

"Have fun baking *kichlin* [cookies]," Jacob called in return. "Oh, and one more thing: *Geb acht, schunscht geht's letz* [Watch out, or else things will go wrong]!"

Rachel gritted her teeth and hurried along. As she approached Grandma and Grandpa's house, she noticed her three-year-old cousin Gerald sitting on the front porch of his house with a jar of bubbles. Gerald and his parents, Aunt Karen and Uncle Amos, had moved into the house next door to Grandma and Grandpa soon after Mary and her family moved to Indiana.

Rachel decided to visit with Gerald a few minutes. Maybe she could blow some bubbles.

"*Blos* [bubble]," Gerald said when Rachel took a seat on the step next to him. He lifted the jar of bubbles.

She smiled. "Can I blow some?"

He nodded and handed her the plastic wand.

Rachel dipped it into the jar and waved it around. A stream of colorful bubbles blew into the yard.

Gerald squealed and clapped his hands. "Blos! Blos! *Geh* [Go]!"

Rachel dipped the wand into the jar again, only this time instead of waving the wand, she blew on it. More bubbles floated into the yard.

"Blos! Blos!" Gerald hollered. He snatched the wand from Rachel and dipped it into the jar. Holding the wand in front of Rachel's face, he blew. A big bubble formed, but before the wind could catch it, Gerald poked it with his finger, and—*pop!*—it burst in Rachel's face!

"Ach, that stings!" she cried as she rubbed her eyes. Rachel blinked several times, trying to clear her vision. "I should have expected something like this to happen," she mumbled. The last time she'd visited Gerald, she'd given him a horsey ride, and he'd smacked her in the eye.

When the stinging stopped, she handed Gerald the jar of bubbles and stood. "I have to go. Grandma's expecting me, and I don't have any more time to play."

Gerald didn't seem to notice as she walked away. He was too busy blowing more bubbles.

Thump! Thump! Thump! Rachel knocked on Grandma's door.

"Come in," Grandma called.

Rachel entered the house and sniffed the delicious odor of cinnamon and molasses. "Did you bake the cookies without me?" she asked when she stepped into the kitchen and found Grandma sitting at the table, reading the newspaper.

Grandma looked up and smiled. "Of course not. I promised that we would bake the cookies together."

Rachel sniffed the air again. "Then why do I smell cinnamon and molasses?"

"That's from the gingerbread I baked earlier today." Grandma pushed the newspaper aside and stood. "Would you like a piece?"

Rachel shook her head. "No thanks. I'll wait until the cookies are done and have some of those."

"All right. Are you ready to begin?" Grandma asked.

Rachel nodded eagerly. "What kind of cookies are we gonna make?"

"How about some maple syrup cookies?" Grandma wiggled her eyebrows. "Those are some of your daed's favorites."

Rachel leaned on the counter. "I didn't know that. No wonder Mom bakes them so often."

Grandma bobbed her head. "I used to make maple syrup cookies at least once a week when your daed was a buwe. I gave your mamm the recipe as soon as they got married."

"I like maple syrup cookies real well, too." Rachel patted her stomach and grinned. "Guess I take after my daed."

"I guess you do." Grandma opened a cupboard door and took down her recipe box. She opened it, pulled out a recipe, and handed it to Rachel. "Why don't you read the recipe and then get out the ingredients, while I preheat the oven?"

"I can do that." Rachel placed the card on the counter and opened the cupboard where Grandma kept her baking supplies. As she studied the recipe, the words looked blurry. *I'll bet I still have some of that bubble Gerald popped in my eye,* she thought.

Rachel ran to the bathroom. She opened both eyes wide and splashed water on her face. *That ought to do it.*

She blinked a few times and looked in the mirror. *Hmm. . .my face even looks blurry. I wonder how long it's been since Grandma cleaned this mirror.*

"Rachel, where are you?" Grandma called.

Rachel dried her face on a towel and ran back to the kitchen. "I was in the bathroom, rinsing my eyes."

Grandma forehead wrinkled. "Is something wrong with your eyes?"

"I was having trouble reading the recipe, and I thought I might have bubble solution in my eyes."

Grandma frowned. "How would you get bubble solution in your eyes?"

"Before I came here, I blew bubbles with Gerald, and he popped one in my face. I think that blurred my vision." Rachel pointed to her eyes. "Even after I rinsed them, my face looked blurry in the bathroom mirror. I wonder if the mirror is dirty, Grandma."

Grandma shook her head. "I cleaned that mirror this morning." She pursed her lips. "Come closer and let me look at your eyes."

Rachel stood in front of Grandma and opened her eyes as widely as she could.

"I don't see anything." Grandma motioned to the recipe card. "Were you having trouble reading the whole recipe, or just a few words?"

"All of it," Rachel admitted. "Could something have gotten spilled on the recipe?"

Grandma ran her fingers over the card. "I don't see or feel anything." She faced Rachel. "Maybe you need a pair of glasses."

Rachel gasped. "Ach, I hope not! I never want to wear glasses!"

"Why not?"

"Because I think they would make me look *schpassich* [odd]. Jacob and the kinner at school might make fun of me if I wore glasses."

Grandma touched the nose piece on her own glasses. "Do you think I look schpassich?"

"Of course not," Rachel said, shaking her head. "I only meant. . . Well, some of the kinner might think I look odd because I've never worn glasses before."

Grandma touched Rachel's chin. "If I were you, I'd be more concerned about seeing well than worrying about what others might think."

Rachel thought about that a few seconds. "Do you like wearing glasses?" she asked.

Grandma nodded. "I don't mind them at all. Fact is, I've worn glasses since I was a teenager. They've become a part of me now. Sometimes I even fall asleep with them on." She chuckled. "I'll never forget the day, soon after I'd turned sixteen, when I forgot I was wearing my glasses."

"What happened?"

"Some of my friends and I had gone to the lake to swim," Grandma said. "I forgot to take my glasses off before I went in the water and almost lost them."

"Did they float away?"

Grandma shook her head. "They started to sink, but I grabbed them in time."

Hearing how Grandma had nearly lost her glasses in the lake made Rachel hope all the more that she would never have to wear glasses. She pointed to the recipe card. "It might be better if you read the recipe and tell me what ingredients I should get from the cupboard."

Grandma smiled. "Jah, okay."

"Oh, and one more thing," Rachel said.

"What's that?"

"Please don't say anything to Mom or Pap about me not being able to read the recipe card. I don't want to worry them."

Grandma tapped her finger against her chin, as

she considered this. "I won't say anything for now, but if your vision continues to blur, then you'd better tell your folks right away."

"Okay," Rachel said, nodding.

"Third and fourth graders, I've written your English assignment on the blackboard," Elizabeth said during school the next day. "I want you to look at the sentences and then write down every noun, verb, and adjective you see."

Rachel leaned forward with her elbows on her desk and studied the sentences her teacher had written. If she squinted, she could read some of the words, but most of them looked fuzzy.

She blinked several times, hoping her eyes would focus, but it was no use. She couldn't see well enough to know what the sentences said.

Rachel leaned across the aisle and whispered, "*Psst. . .* Audra. . .can you read those sentences?"

Audra nodded. "Of course I can."

"What do they say?"

Audra's eyebrows pulled together as she stared at Rachel. "Can't you read them?"

"Well, I—"

"No talking, please!" Elizabeth's stern voice caused Rachel to jump.

Rachel raised her hand.

"What is it, Rachel?" Elizabeth asked.

"The words on the board look kind of blurry, and I was asking Audra if she knew what they said."

"Rachel, please come here," Elizabeth said. "We need to talk."

Rachel's cheeks burned with embarrassment when she noticed that everyone in class seemed to be looking at her. She wished she hadn't said anything. She wished she could crawl under her desk and stay there until school was over.

Rachel shuffled to the front of the room.

Elizabeth leaned close to Rachel. "Now what's all this about blurry words on the blackboard?"

"I—I can't tell wh–what all the words say," Rachel stammered as she wiped her sweaty hands on her skirt.

"Have you had trouble seeing other things?" Elizabeth questioned.

Rachel thought about the letter from Mary and the recipe card at Grandma's. She hadn't been able to read either one of those. She remembered the baseball that had looked like a white blur; the spider and the butterfly she hadn't been able to see; and the bird that had looked like a blurry blob. A knot formed in her throat. Maybe something *was* wrong with her eyes. Maybe she *would* end up wearing glasses whether she liked it or not.

"Rachel, did you hear my question?"

"Jah."

"Have you had trouble seeing other things?"

Rachel nodded slowly, and her throat felt so swollen she could hardly swallow.

Elizabeth reached into her desk and withdrew a notebook. She wrote something on the paper and handed it to Rachel. "This is a note for your parents. I'm letting them know that you're having trouble seeing the letters on the blackboard. I've suggested they make an appointment to get your eyes examined."

Thump! Thumpety! Thump! Thump! Rachel's heart hammered in her chest. She'd never had her eyes examined before. Would it hurt? Would the doctor be nice? Would he make her wear glasses? If he did, would the glasses cost a lot of money? So many questions swirled around in her head that she could hardly think.

"I'll move your desk closer to the blackboard so you can see better," Elizabeth said.

As Elizabeth pushed Rachel's desk to the front of the room, Rachel made a decision. She would hide the note from Mom and Pap so she wouldn't have to see the doctor. Even if she had to keep her desk at the front of the room for the rest of the school year, it would be better than wearing glasses!

That night at supper, Rachel stared at her plate of

fried chicken, mashed potatoes, and pickled red beets. These were some of her favorite foods, but she didn't feel like eating. She could only think about the note at the bottom of her backpack.

"You're awfully quiet," Grandpa said, touching Rachel's arm.

"She hasn't eaten much supper, either," Henry added.

"Are you feeling grank?" Mom asked, looking at Rachel with concern.

Rachel shifted in her seat, unsure of what to say. "I'm not sick." She took a bite of chicken, but it tasted like cardboard, and she had a hard time swallowing.

"I'll bet she's thinking about that note our teacher gave her today," Jacob said.

Rachel glared at him. If he were sitting closer she might have kicked him under the table.

"What note?" asked Pap, looking at Rachel.

Rachel felt like a glob of peanut butter was stuck in her throat. She reached for her glass of water and took a drink.

"What note?" Pap asked again.

Rachel set the glass on the table and blew out her breath. "Elizabeth thinks I should have my eyes examined."

Mom stared at Rachel over her glasses. "What makes her think that?"

"Well, uh—the words on the blackboard looked kind of blurry today, and I—uh—couldn't tell what they said."

Pap stared at Rachel so hard her toes curled inside her sneakers. "When were you planning to give us the note?"

Rachel moistened her lips with the tip of her tongue. "Well, I—"

"I'll bet she wasn't going to give you the note," Jacob said. "I'll bet she—"

Mom held up her hand and frowned at Jacob. "You'd best stay out of this, son." She turned to Rachel. "If Elizabeth thinks you should have your eyes examined, I'll call the eye doctor tomorrow and make an appointment." She shook her finger at Rachel. "The next time your teacher gives you a note, I expect you to give it to me right away. Is that clear?"

Rachel nodded as tears pooled in her eyes, making everything on the table look blurry. "I'm not hungry," she mumbled, struggling not to cry. "May—may I be excused?"

Mom gave a quick nod. "But remember, there will be no dessert if you don't finish your supper."

"I don't care about dessert!" Rachel sucked in a huge sob, pushed back her chair, and raced from the room. "I don't want to wear glasses! I'd rather see blurry words for the rest of my life!"

She dashed up the stairs two at a time. *Thunk!*— she tripped on the last step and dropped to her knees.

Rachel grabbed the railing and pulled herself up, as tears coursed down her cheeks. "Trouble, trouble. . . there's always trouble somewhere!"

Chapter 6

Learning the Truth

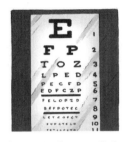

Rachel stared out the window of their driver's van and tried to concentrate on the scenery going by—anything to keep from thinking about where they were going. *Zip! Zip! Zip!* It felt as if a bunch of butterflies were flying around in her stomach.

Mom had made an appointment for Rachel to see the eye doctor today. She'd hired their English neighbor, Susan Johnson, to take them to Lancaster for the appointment. Susan had picked them up as soon as Rachel got home from school. Rachel wished she could be anywhere but here. Even doing chores would be better than getting her eyes examined.

"Don't look so *naerfich* [nervous]." Mom gently squeezed Rachel's arm. "The doctor's just going to look at your eyes."

"And probably make me wear glasses," Rachel mumbled.

"We won't know that until after the examination.

Besides, wearing glasses isn't so bad." Mom pushed her glasses onto the bridge of her nose. "Without my glasses I wouldn't be able to see nearly as well. Grandma Yoder wears glasses, too," she added with a smile. "And Grandpa Schrock needs glasses for reading."

"I know that, but no one at school wears glasses. If the doctor says I have to wear them, I'll be the only scholar with glasses." Rachel swallowed hard. "Wearing glasses would make me stick out like a sore thumb!"

"You won't stick out like a sore thumb." Mom patted Rachel's knee. "Even if no one else wears glasses now, it doesn't mean they never will."

Rachel leaned back in her seat and closed her eyes. She tried to imagine how some of her friends would look with glasses. Would they wear the metal-framed kind like Mom, Grandma Yoder, and Grandpa Schrock wore; or would they wear colored plastic frames like she'd seen on other folks? She almost giggled when she pictured Orlie wearing a pair of glasses with thick lenses that made him look like a frog.

Audra's brother, Brian, had a round face, so if he wore glasses, he might look like a pumpkin. Phoebe Byler's nose was thin, and she had small, beady eyes, so if she wore glasses she'd probably look like a bird.

Mom nudged Rachel's arm. "We're here!"

Rachel's eyes popped open. The butterflies in her stomach started zipping again.

Rachel and Mom sat in the doctor's waiting room.

Mom read a magazine. Rachel took deep breaths and tried to relax. It was easy for Mom to say there was nothing to be nervous about; she wasn't the one getting her eyes examined today. She wasn't the one who might get teased if she wore glasses at school, either.

A middle-aged woman with short red hair stepped up to Rachel. "My name is Mrs. Dodge, and I'm the doctor's assistant. Will you please come with me?"

Rachel stood and wiped her sweaty palms on her dress. "Will you come with me?" she asked Mom.

Mom nodded. "Of course."

Rachel and Mom followed Mrs. Dodge into another room. She motioned to a chair that looked similar to the one Rachel sat in the last time she'd gone to the dentist—only this chair had a strange-looking machine in front of it.

Mrs. Dodge asked Rachel several questions: how old she was; had she ever worn glasses; was she having any trouble with her eyes; and had she ever had an eye exam. When she finished her questions, she looked at Rachel and said, "Now look straight ahead at the chart on the wall. Do you see some groups of letters?"

Rachel nodded. "I see them, but some are fuzzy."

"That's okay. Just read the smallest line that you're able to see clearly."

"The top line looks the clearest," Rachel said.

"That's fine. Please read the letters on that line."

"F, E, L, O, P, Z, D."

"Can you read the next line?"

"D. . .No, I think that's an O." Rachel squinted as she concentrated on each letter. "F. . .No, that's an E. Well, maybe it is an F. I—I can't really be sure."

Mrs. Dodge plucked a bottle from the shelf across the room, and moved closer to Rachel. "Hold your head still. I'm going to put some drops in your eyes."

Rachel flinched. "Wh—why do I need drops in my eyes?"

"The drops are to dilate your eyes," Mrs. Dodge explained. "Dilating makes the pupils larger and helps the doctor see the backs of your eyes."

"Why does he need to look at the backs of my eyes?" Rachel wanted to know.

"To see if there's any swelling or disease."

Rachel didn't think her eyes were swollen, and she hoped they had no disease. "W—will the eye drops hurt?" she asked shakily.

"They might sting a little, but the stinging sensation won't last long."

Mom took hold of Rachel's hand. "It's okay. Just relax."

Rachel drew in a deep breath, leaned her head against the back of the chair, and tried not to blink.

Squirt. Squirt. "There now; you did just fine," Mrs. Dodge said. "The doctor will be in to see you soon."

She handed Rachel a tissue and scurried out of the room.

Rachel dabbed at her watery eyes. "What's this for, Mom?" she asked, pointing to the big machine in front of her.

Mom sat in a chair near the door. "When the doctor comes in he'll have you look at the eye chart again, only this time you'll be looking through the large lenses attached to the machine. He'll also look at your eyes with a bright light."

"Will the bright light hurt?"

"No, Rachel." Mom smiled. "Now please sit back and relax."

Rachel closed her eyes and sighed, wishing the doctor would hurry. The longer she waited, the more nervous she became. She opened her eyes and fiddled with the strings on her kapp, knowing Mom would scold her if she bit a fingernail.

Finally, the door squeaked open. A tall man wearing metal-framed glasses entered the room. "Hello, Rachel. I'm Dr. Ben. I understand you're having some trouble with your eyes."

"Well, uh—some things look a little blurry lately, but I hope I won't need to wear glasses."

He touched the earpiece of his glasses; then rubbed his chin. "Do you have something against glasses?"

She swallowed a couple of times. "Not really. I just

think I'm too young to wear them."

Dr. Ben winked at Mom. Then he sat on the stool near the front of the strange-looking machine. "Now let's take a look at your eyes so I can see what's going on."

"W—will it hurt?"

"No, Rachel, I'm just going to examine your eyes." The doctor shined a bright light into Rachel's eyes. It didn't hurt, but it was hard to keep her eyes open.

Then Dr. Ben positioned the machine in front of Rachel's face. "Now lean forward so your forehead is resting against the machine and your chin is on the chin rest."

Rachel did as he asked. The exam included a lot more than she'd expected, but so far it had been easy enough.

"Do you see the eye chart through the lenses, Rachel?"

"Yes."

"I'll adjust the lenses," Dr. Ben said. "I want you to let me know if you can see the letters any better." *Click! Click!*

"Oh, yes, they're much clearer now," she said as the letters came into focus.

Click! Click! The doctor made a few more adjustments. "Is this better?"

"I—I think the first one was better."

"How about this?" He changed the lenses a few more times, always asking Rachel which one was better.

Finally, he pulled the machine away from her face.

"We're all done." He looked over at Mom and said, "Rachel's eyes have a slight astigmatism."

"Astigmatism," Rachel repeated. "What's that?"

"It's when the front surface of the eye is shaped like an egg," Dr. Ben explained.

Rachel frowned. She had no idea her eye looked like an egg.

"When a person has astigmatism, it can affect vision and distort shapes so letters and numbers that look similar are often confused." Dr. Ben looked over at Mom again. "Rachel is also farsighted in one eye and nearsighted in the other."

"What does farsighted and nearsighted mean?" Rachel asked.

"Farsighted is an eye condition that makes it hard for you to see things that are close. Nearsighted means you have a hard time seeing things that are far away."

Tears pricked the backs of Rachel's eyes as the doctor's words sank in. Something *was* wrong with her eyes, and she *would* have to wear glasses. She'd probably never be able to see well without them.

Dr. Ben patted Rachel's shoulder. "Once you get your glasses you'll be able to see everything much better." He wrote something on a small notepad and handed it to Mom. "Here's the prescription for Rachel's new glasses."

Mom nodded. "Thank you, Dr. Ben."

Rachel swallowed. She wanted to see better, but she didn't want glasses!

Dr. Ben motioned to the door. "You can go next door to the optical department and give them the prescription for Rachel's glasses. Then she can pick out a nice pair of frames."

The butterflies in Rachel's stomach started zipping around again. The tears she'd been holding back flooded her eyes, making her vision even more blurry. "Are—are you sure I have to get glasses?"

He nodded. "But if you wear them all the time for the next few years, maybe your eyes will get stronger and you won't have to wear them at all."

Hope welled in Rachel's chest. "Really?"

He nodded and handed her a pair of cardboard glasses with dark lenses. "The dilation will last for several hours, and your eyes will be sensitive to light, so put these on before you go outside."

Rachel grimaced. She couldn't get out of it; she would have to wear glasses. She just hoped it wouldn't be forever.

"Do you want plastic frames or metal frames?" Mom asked when she and Rachel entered the optical shop.

Rachel shrugged.

"Let's look at some plastic frames. I think those will look good on you." Mom led Rachel to the wall where rows of glasses with plastic frames hung. Rachel could hardly tell how they looked because her eyes were blurrier than normal from the dilation.

"What do you think of these?" Mom asked, lifting a pair of glasses. "They're a nice of shade of blue, and they'll match your pretty eyes. What do you think, Rachel?"

"I—I guess they'll be all right." Rachel swallowed a couple of times and drew in a deep breath. She didn't want to cry right here in the optical shop.

A short man with thinning brown hair stepped up to them. "May I help you?"

Mom handed him the prescription Dr. Ben had given her. "My daughter needs new glasses, and we think this pair would look nice."

Rachel just stared at the floor.

"Let's go over to the table so I can get some measurements and see how the glasses look on your face," the man said.

Rachel flopped into a chair in front of the table. She didn't care what color the glasses were or how well they looked on her face. She wished she could turn back the hands of time—back to when she could see everything clearly and didn't need glasses.

Later that afternoon, Rachel sat on the porch swing, thinking about her eye examination, and about the frames Mom had picked for her.

In just one week I'll have my new glasses, she thought. *I hope I'll like them. I hope no one at school will make fun of me.*

Rachel thought about what Mom had said about the frames. *I'll bet Mom was only trying to make me feel better when she said the new glasses would match my eyes.* She pushed the swing back and forth and tried to relax.

Bzzz. . .Bzzz. Rachel recognized the sound. Even though she only saw a little blur, she knew a bee was buzzing near her head.

Bzzz. . .Bzzz. . .Bzzz. She didn't want to get stung, so she swatted at the bee.

"Ouch!" Rachel bumped her elbow on the back of the swing, and a tingling pain shot up her arm.

Bzzz. . .Bzzz. The pesky bee continued to buzz her head.

Rachel jumped up, raced for the door, and stumbled over one of Mom's flowerpots. "Trouble, trouble, trouble," she muttered.

The back door swung open. "Oh, Rachel, I was just coming to get you," Mom said. "Supper's almost ready, and the table needs to be set."

Rachel hurried into the kitchen and slammed the door. At least she was away from that buzzing bee!

Mom motioned to the refrigerator. "After you put

the dishes and silverware on the table you can set out the iced tea. And could you also get the sour cream? It's in a plastic bowl in the refrigerator."

"Okay, Mom."

"Oh, and when you're done with that, please fill the sugar bowl. The sugar is in the cupboard."

Rachel opened the silverware drawer and took out the knives, forks, and spoons. As she placed them on the table, she thought about making a game of it, but wasn't in the mood. When she finished setting the table, she went to the refrigerator and took out the iced tea and the container of sour cream. Then she filled the sugar bowl and had just set it on the table when Pap, Henry, Jacob, and Grandpa entered the kitchen.

"Mmm. . .something smells mighty good." Grandpa combed his beard with his fingers and sniffed the air.

"I'll bet Mom made meatloaf tonight," Henry said. "I'd recognize that *wunderbaar* [wonderful] smell any-where."

"You're right, Henry," Mom said, smiling. "I made your favorite supper."

Rachel frowned. It didn't seem fair that Mom had fixed Henry's favorite dish. Rachel was the one who'd had a rough day. Mom should have fixed her favorite meal—fried chicken, potato salad, biscuits with jam, and pickled beets.

"Supper's on the table," Mom said. "So, let's sit down."

Henry grinned and patted his stomach. "And we'll eat 'til we're full!"

"After we pray, of course," Pap said, nodding.

Everyone took seats at the table, and all heads bowed for prayer.

"Dear Lord," Rachel silently prayed, *"I don't like the idea of wearing glasses, but I did like Dr. Ben; he seemed real nice. When I get my new glasses next week, help me get used to wearing them. . . . And please don't let anyone at school make fun of me."*

When Pap cleared his throat, Rachel opened her eyes and sipped her water.

Henry cut his baked potato in half and put a pat of butter in the center. "Would you pass me the sour cream, Rachel?"

Rachel handed the bowl to Henry. He spooned some onto his potato, took a big bite, and puckered his lips. "This isn't sour cream; it's whipping cream!" He frowned at Rachel. "Did you set the table?"

She nodded and her cheeks burned with embarrassment. She'd obviously made a mistake.

"Why'd you put out whipping cream instead of sour cream?" Henry asked. "What were you thinking?"

"I—I didn't do it on purpose. My eyes are still dilated, and everything looks real blurry."

Henry scraped the whipping cream off his baked potato, stomped to the refrigerator, took out another plastic bowl, and tromped back. "Now this is sour cream," he said, spooning some onto his potato.

Rachel's head started hurting. She rubbed her forehead with her fingertips.

"Would someone please pass the sugar?" Grandpa asked. "I like my iced tea a little sweeter."

Mom handed him the sugar bowl.

"Danki." Grandpa put two teaspoons of sugar in his glass of iced tea, stirred it, and took a drink. His lips puckered, his nose twitched, and his eyebrows pulled together. "What happened to this iced tea? It tastes salty."

Mom picked up the sugar bowl, spooned a little onto her plate, and took a bite. She looked at Rachel. "When I asked you to fill the sugar bowl, I meant with sugar, not salt."

Rachel's face grew hotter as she slumped in her chair. "The writing on the bag looked blurry. It—it must have been salt, and I thought it was sugar."

Grandpa reached over and patted Rachel's arm. "It's okay. Everything will be better once you get your new glasses. Then things won't look blurry anymore."

Rachel blinked against the tears stinging her eyes. She hoped Grandpa was right. She needed to believe things would soon be better.

After the supper dishes were done, Rachel asked Mom

if she could go to the barn to play with Cuddles.

"I guess it would be all right," Mom said. "But don't stay out there too long. It'll be bedtime soon."

"Okay, Mom." Rachel scurried out the back door.

She dashed across the yard, eased the barn door open, and peeked inside. The familiar smells comforted her—grain, hay, dust, and even the strong animal odors.

Rachel spotted Cuddles sleeping on a bale of hay. She hurried to pick up the cat. Cuddles purred and nestled against Rachel's chest.

"I have to wear glasses, Cuddles," Rachel complained. "I'm going to get them next week, and I'm not happy about it." Her shoulders rose and fell as she struggled not to cry.

Meow. Cuddles opened one eye and looked up at Rachel as if to say, "I'm sorry you're unhappy. I'm still your friend."

Rachel sat with the cat in her lap, surrounded by a restful silence. Even as a kitten, Cuddles had often offered Rachel comfort.

Rachel yawned, stretched, and wiggled her bare toes, as a silent prayer floated through her mind. *Dear God: Danki for Cuddles.*

Chapter 7

Four Eyes

Rachel stared out the window of Susan Johnson's van. She and Mom were on their way to pick up her new glasses, and butterflies zipped around in her stomach again.

What if the glasses didn't help her see better? What if she didn't like how she looked in them? What if Jacob and the kids at school made fun of her?

Rachel was about to chomp off the end of a nail, when Mom reached for her hand. "No nail biting, Rachel."

"Sorry, Mom, but I'm feeling naerfich." Rachel touched her stomach. "It feels like butterflies are fluttering around in here."

"Are you nervous about getting your glasses?"
Rachel nodded.

"Don't be nervous. Why, once you get your glasses and can see things better, you'll be happy as a lamb."

"I hope so." Rachel tapped her foot and squirmed.

Mom squeezed Rachel's fingers. "Try to think of something else so you won't feel naerfich. Think of something pleasant—something you enjoy."

Rachel let her head fall against the seat and closed her eyes. She thought about her cuddly cat. She thought about their old horse, Tom, and how he seemed glad to see her whenever she visited him in the pasture or barn. She thought about her cousin Mary and all the fun things they used to do. She thought about the coming summer and how she looked forward to spending time with Audra. She hoped Audra could come over to her house and jump on the trampoline. Maybe she could go over to Audra's and skateboard in the barn. She thought about wading in the creek behind their house and picnics at the pond down the road. She could do so many fun things in the summer.

"We're here," Mom said, nudging Rachel's arm.

Rachel's eyes snapped open. The dreaded moment had arrived: Time to get her glasses.

When they entered the optical shop, the man who'd waited on Rachel the week before asked her to sit in front of a table. He brought out the pair of glasses with light blue frames that Mom had chosen for Rachel. He smiled and slipped them on Rachel's face, checking to be sure they fit on the bridge of her nose and behind her ears.

"Can you see better now?" he asked, handing her a small chart with some words on it.

Rachel blinked as she stared at the chart. She could hardly believe it! The letters were so clear and bright. They seemed to jump right off the page!

"Can you see the words clearly?" he asked.

She nodded.

"Would you like to see how you look in your new glasses?"

"Yes."

He handed her a small mirror.

Rachel gasped at her reflection. She hardly recognized the girl looking back at her! She turned to Mom and asked, "What do you think?"

Mom smiled. "I think your new glasses look very nice. In fact, I think you look quite grown up."

"Really?"

"Jah."

Rachel grinned at her reflection. Maybe the glasses did make her look older. They sure helped her see better. Maybe wearing glasses wouldn't be so bad after all.

When they left the optical shop, Rachel couldn't stop grinning. Everything outside looked so crisp and clear. The sun looked brighter; the sky looked bluer; the trees looked greener. She stared at the clouds and studied the different shapes. She hadn't even realized how many things she hadn't been able to see well before.

Looking through her new glasses was like seeing the world in a brand-new light. She was sure she'd be able to see the blackboard and the words in her schoolbooks better, too.

"Can we stop by Esther and Rudy's on the way home?" Rachel asked Mom as they climbed into Susan's van. "I'd like to show them my new glasses."

"I suppose we could stop for a few minutes if Susan has the time," Mom said.

"I have plenty of time, and I'd be happy to take you to Esther and Rudy's," Susan called over her shoulder.

"Danki, we appreciate that." Mom smiled at Rachel. "Rudy might be working in the fields today, but I'm sure Esther will enjoy seeing your new glasses."

When Susan's van pulled in front of Esther and Rudy's house, Rachel spotted Esther sitting in a chair on her front porch. Rachel hurried up the sidewalk ahead of Mom and Susan.

Esther smiled when Rachel stepped onto the porch. "Look at you, little schweschder. You have new glasses!"

Rachel nodded. "Do you like them?"

"Jah, very much. They're a pretty color, and they make you look so grown up."

"That's what Mom said, too."

Esther hugged Rachel. "Can you see better now?"

"Oh, jah. Everything looks so bright and clear. No more blurry vision for me," Rachel said, shaking her head.

"I'm glad."

"*Wie geht's* [How are you], Esther?" Mom asked as she and Susan stepped onto the porch.

Esther smiled and touched her stomach. "Other than a little morning sickness, I'm doing quite well."

"That's good to hear." Mom patted her own stomach. "I'm not having bouts of morning sickness at all anymore. I'm sure it will be over for you soon, too."

"I hope so, because I don't want to feel sick to my stomach the whole time I'm waiting for my baby to be born."

Mom shook her head. "I'm sure you won't."

Esther smiled at Susan. "Thank you for bringing Rachel by so she could show me her new glasses."

Susan smiled and touched her own plastic-framed glasses. "I saw how excited Rachel was when she came out of the optical shop. I felt the same way when I got my first pair of glasses."

"How old were you when you got glasses?" Rachel asked.

"I was twelve years old."

Rachel's heart felt like it had sunk all the way to her toes. *If Susan began wearing glasses when she was a girl, and she's still wearing them now, does that mean I'll be wearing glasses when I become a woman?* she wondered. *Maybe Dr. Ben only told me I might not have to always wear them to make me feel better. Maybe I'll have to wear glasses the rest of my life.*

"I made fresh lemonade. Would you care for some?" Esther asked.

"That sounds good," Mom said.

Susan and Rachel nodded.

"I'll go inside and bring it out," Esther said.

"Do you need help?" Mom asked.

"That's all right; I can manage." Esther went into the house and returned a few minutes later with a pitcher of lemonade and four paper cups.

"Umm. . .this is refreshing." Susan smiled. "Thank you, Esther."

"You're welcome." Esther moved over to the porch swing and was about to sit, when Rudy rushed out of the barn, hollering and waving his hands. "Come back here, you silly *gees* [goat]!"

Ma-a-a! Ma-a-a! The goat leaped over the laundry basket under Esther's clothesline, and darted across the lawn. Rudy's feet slipped on the grass, and he nearly fell, but righted himself and continued the chase.

Rachel thought Rudy might need some help, so she hopped off the porch and raced after the goat.

The frisky critter zipped under Rudy's legs, circled

twice around Rachel, and headed back toward the laundry basket. Rachel lunged for the goat, but it slipped through her hands, and she fell on her knees. "Ach, stupid gees!" she shouted.

Ma-a-a-a! The goat backed up and stood there, as if taunting her.

Rachel clambered to her feet and lunged again, but the goat darted toward Rudy.

Ma-a-a! Ma-a-a! Ma-a-a!

Rudy sprinted to the left. Rachel scuttled to the right. Mom, Esther, and Susan stood on the porch cheering them on. Suddenly, the goat scampered to Rachel and stopped.

She squinted. For some reason the goat looked blurry. She blinked a couple of times and reached up to touch her glasses. They were gone!

Rachel gasped. "My glasses! Where are my glasses?"

"Be careful!" Mom shouted. "Your glasses are on the ground behind you!"

Rachel turned, and—*wham!*—she was knocked to the ground.

"*Dumm* [dumb] gees," she muttered, realizing the goat had butted her.

Rudy grabbed the goat. "Are you all right, Rachel?"

"I—I'm okay." She scooped up her glasses and scrambled to her feet.

"I'm real sorry," Rudy said. "That mischievous goat

never misses an opportunity to butt someone."

Mom left the porch and rushed across the lawn. "Ach, I hope your glasses aren't broken!"

"I—I think they're okay." Rachel handed them to Mom.

Mom studied the glasses and smiled. "Thankfully, they're fine." She gave them back to Rachel. "Maybe I can rig up an elastic strap that connects to the earpiece and fits around the back of your head so you won't lose your glasses when you're outside playing."

Rachel wrinkled her nose. She didn't like the sound of that. Even if the children at school didn't make fun of her glasses, someone—probably Jacob—would surely tease her if she wore a strange strap around the back of her head. "No Mom, please!" she said. "I'll be careful not to let my glasses fall off my face."

"We can talk about this later," Mom said. "We need to get home so I can start supper."

Rachel nodded. After that wild goat chase, she was more than ready to go home.

When Susan pulled up to the house, Rachel thanked her, climbed out, and hurried inside while Mom paid for the ride. Rachel could hardly wait to show her new glasses to everyone in the family. She hoped they liked them as much as Mom and Esther did.

She spotted Grandpa in the rocking chair in the

living room. His eyes were closed and she wondered if he was asleep.

When she stepped into the room, he opened his eyes and greeted her with a smile. He leaned forward so fast the rocker almost tipped him out. "Your glasses look real nice, Rachel. Can you see better now?"

She nodded. "When I'm wearing them, nothing looks blurry."

"That's good to hear. It's not fun to have blurry vision."

"You only wear glasses for reading, right?"

Grandpa nodded. "Have for a good many years."

"The eye doctor said if I wear my glasses for a couple of years, I might not have to wear them all the time." Rachel frowned. "I'm worried that he might have just said that to make me feel better, though. What if I have to wear them for the rest of my life?"

"That wouldn't be so bad," he said. "Your mamm's worn glasses for a good many years, and she's never complained."

Rachel glanced at Mom, who'd just stepped into the living room.

"Sorry we're late," Mom said. "We stopped by Esther's so she could see Rachel's glasses, and then Rachel and Rudy got involved in a wild goat chase."

Grandpa chuckled. "I've chased plenty of goats in my day, I'll tell you. Always left me feeling plenty *mied* [tired]."

Rachel nodded. "I was feeling meid after our goat chase, too."

"That's how it usually is after a good goat chase." Grandpa tugged his earlobe. "I remember one day when I was boy, my daed's old billy goat stole my hat and chewed off the brim. So I took out after him and we ran around the yard so many times we made a path in the grass."

Mom clucked her tongue. "Ach, how you exaggerate, Dad."

"I'm not exaggerating." Grandpa shook his head. "That story really happened, just the way I told it."

"Did you ever catch the goat?" Rachel asked.

"Sure did. I caught him out behind the barn, when he was trying to get through the fence." Grandpa pulled his other earlobe. "Silly goat ended up getting his head caught instead."

Rachel snickered. It was nice to know she wasn't the only one who'd ever had trouble with a goat.

Just then, the back door squeaked open, and Pap entered the room.

"Hi, Pap. Do you notice anything new about me?" Rachel asked, stepping up to him.

He studied her a few seconds and smiled. "Are you wearing a new dress?"

She shook her head.

He glanced down at her feet. "New shoes?"

"*Nee* [No]. They're the same shoes I had on this morning."

"Hmm. . ." Pap stroked his beard, then rubbed the bridge of his nose. "Now I wonder what could be new with my Rachel today?"

Mom poked Pap's arm and rolled her eyes. "Your daughter got her new glasses this afternoon, Levi."

Pap leaned closer to Rachel, studied her for a few seconds, and grinned. "Well, well. . .so you did. Those glasses are nice, Rachel. Jah, very nice indeed."

"What's very nice?" Henry asked when he entered the room.

"Your sister's new glasses." Pap motioned to Rachel. "Come see what you think."

Henry moved over to Rachel. "I see you picked out some blue ones to match your eyes."

She nodded. "Do you think they look all right?"

"They look more than all right. They look *fehlerfrie* [perfect] for you."

Rachel smiled. "Danki, Henry."

Jacob stepped into the room. "I'm finished with my chores. How soon 'til supper?"

"It'll be a while," Mom said. "Rachel and I were at the optical shop, and then we stopped by Esther and Rudy's to show them her new glasses."

Jacob squinted at Rachel.

"What do you think?" she asked.

"I didn't realize your glasses would be so thick." Jacob's lips turned up at the corners. "Ha! Now you have four eyes instead of two!"

"What?" Rachel's chin trembled, and her eyes filled with tears.

Mom frowned at Jacob. "Apologize to your sister for saying such a mean thing."

"Your mamm's right," Pap put in. "That remark was uncalled for, and not even true."

"Sorry, Rachel," Jacob mumbled.

Rachel didn't reply. She raced to the bathroom and looked in the mirror. *Do I really look like I have four eyes? If I do, I don't see how I can go to school tomorrow. I'll have to come up with a good reason to stay home.*

Chapter 8

Jacob's Promise

Bam! Bam! Bam! "Mom wants you downstairs for breakfast!" Jacob called as he banged on Rachel's bedroom door. "If we don't eat now we'll be late for school!"

Rachel pulled the covers over her head.

"Schnell, Rachel! Schnell!"

"Okay, okay. I'll be there soon." Rachel climbed out of bed and hurried to get dressed. She still hadn't come up with a good reason to stay home from school today, but she hoped she could think of something during breakfast.

Or maybe, she thought as she slipped into her shoes, *I won't wear my glasses at school.*

Rachel left her glasses lying on her dresser, hurried from her room, and rushed downstairs.

"*Guder mariye* [Good morning]," Mom said when Rachel entered the kitchen. "We're ready to eat, so have a seat at the table."

Rachel pulled out the chair beside Grandpa and sat down.

Pap looked at Rachel and frowned. "Where are your glasses?"

"I—I left them in my room."

Mom placed a bowl of oatmeal in front of Rachel. "Be sure you get them right after breakfast."

Rachel fiddled with the edge of her napkin. "Maybe I—uh—shouldn't wear them today."

"Why not?" Pap asked. "You're supposed to wear them all the time, right?"

"Jah, but—" Rachel could barely speak around the lump in her throat. She took a drink of milk. "What if the kinner laugh at me the way Jacob did last night? What if someone calls me four eyes?"

"I'm sure no one at school will tease you about your glasses," Mom said, sitting on the other side of Rachel. "Elizabeth would never allow such a thing." She looked at Jacob and frowned. "You'd better not tease your sister about wearing glasses again."

"Okay, Mom," Jacob said with a nod.

"What if someone teases me during recess when Elizabeth's not there to hear?" Rachel asked.

"Then you should find the teacher and tell her what was said," Henry spoke up.

"If I do that, the kinner will call me a *retschbeddi* [tattletale]."

Jacob looked at Rachel and wrinkled his nose. "That's because you *are* a retschbeddi."

"Am not."

"Are so."

"Am not."

"Are so."

"Am—"

"That will be enough!" Pap said loudly. "Now bow your heads for silent prayer, and be sure when you pray that you make things right with God for arguing with each other this morning."

As Rachel headed to school, wearing her glasses, she noticed the colorful flowers along the way. She wished she had time to stop and pick a few.

She looked at the fluffy clouds floating lazily overhead. It would be nice to lie in the grass and study the shapes of the clouds.

When they came to a tree where some birds were singing, Rachel stopped and listened to their melody.

Jacob nudged her arm. "Hurry up, slowpoke. You're gonna make us late to school if you don't keep walking."

"I am walking."

"No you're not. You've been looking at the sky and stopping every few minutes to smell the flowers."

"I haven't been smelling the flowers; I've only looked at them."

"Whatever you say, little bensel."

Rachel frowned. "Mom said you weren't supposed to tease me."

"I wasn't teasing." Jacob kicked a pebble with the toe of his boot. "You *are* a little bensel."

"I am not a silly child, and you'd better stop calling me that!"

"I will, when you stop acting like one." Jacob walked faster. "See you at school!"

When Rachel arrived at the schoolhouse, the bell was already ringing. She hurried inside and put her lunch pail on the shelf.

"I see you got new glasses," Orlie said. "They sure make you look different."

"Different in a good way?" she asked hopefully.

Orlie shrugged and grinned. "I think they make you look like you've got four eyes." He looked at Audra's brother, Brian, and said, "Don't you think Rachel looks like she has four eyes?"

Brian stared at Rachel a few seconds; then he looked back at Orlie. "I think her glasses look like *schlang aage* [snake eyes]."

Rachel clenched her fingers. "Have you two been talking to Jacob?"

Orlie shook his head. "Huh-uh."

Audra put her lunch pail on the shelf beside Rachel's.

"Don't listen to Orlie and Brian. They just like to tease." She patted Rachel's arm. "I think your glasses are nice. They make you look grown up and real *schmaert* [smart]."

"Do you really think they make me look smart?"

Audra nodded. "Sure do."

Brian nudged Audra's arm. "That's *lecherich* [ridiculous]. Glasses don't make a person look smart. They just tell the world you can't see."

"I'm sure Rachel can see real well now that she's got glasses," Audra said.

"Isn't that true, Rachel?"

Rachel nodded. She was glad Audra had stuck up for her, but after the comments Brian, Orlie, and Jacob had made, she didn't feel smart or grown up. She felt ugly in her glasses. Maybe she shouldn't wear them at school anymore. Maybe she should only wear them at home.

After lunch, Rachel went outside for recess. She spotted Jacob and some other boys sitting on one end of the fence. Orlie was there, too, only he stood on the other end of the fence—his left foot on one railing—his right foot on the railing above.

"*Bass uff as du net fallscht* [Take care you don't fall]," Rachel told him.

He grinned. "Don't worry, I won't."

"I thought I wouldn't fall from the tree when I

tried to rescue Cuddles," she said, "but remember what happened?"

He nodded. "You broke your arm."

"That's right, and if you fall you might break something, too."

"Ah, you worry too much. I know what I'm doing." Orlie wrinkled his freckled nose. "And just because you're wearing glasses that make you look scholarly doesn't mean you're smarter than me."

Rachel shook her head—one quick shake, and then another. "I don't think I'm smarter; I'm just saying you could get hurt if you're not careful."

His lips twitched with a smile, and he puffed out his chest. "Want to see me stand on one leg?"

"No."

"Well, here I go!" Orlie pulled his left leg up so he stood with both legs on the top railing. Then, holding his arms straight out to keep his balance, he lifted his right leg.

Rachel's heart thumped in her chest as Orlie wobbled. She glanced over to see if Jacob saw what Orlie had done, but he was talking to Brian and didn't seem to notice.

"Orlie, please come down from there," she pleaded.

"Aw, quit worrying; I'm doin' fine." He switched to the other leg, and—*whoosh!*—tumbled right to the ground.

Rachel's heart pounded. She rushed forward and dropped beside Orlie. "Are you okay?"

Orlie stared at her, his mouth opening and closing like a fish out of water.

The boys who'd been sitting on the fence hopped down and crowded around Orlie.

"Are you hurt?"

"Did you break anything?"

"Should we get the teacher?"

Everyone spoke at once.

Orlie grunted and pulled himself to a sitting position. "I—I'm okay. Just had the wind knocked out of me."

Rachel clucked her tongue, the way Mom often did, and shook her finger at Orlie. "I told you standing on the fence was a bad idea. You're lucky you weren't hurt. You'd better not do that again."

Orlie stood and brushed the dirt from his trousers. "You're not my mamm, Rachel. You have no right to be tellin' me what to do." *Aaa-choo!* He sneezed.

"When you do foolish things, someone needs to tell you about it." Rachel looked at Jacob. "Standing on the fence with one leg is dumm, isn't it?"

Jacob shrugged. "If Orlie wants to stand on the fence with one leg or two, that's up to him." He pointed at Rachel. "You, little bensel, should mind your own business!"

Hot tears pushed against Rachel's eyelids, and

she gritted her teeth. Why couldn't Jacob stick up for her—especially when he should know she was right?

Rachel whirled around and walked away. Maybe swinging would make her feel better.

"Where ya goin'?" Orlie called after her.

Rachel kept walking.

"She's probably going to look for some flowers to smell." Jacob snickered. "Now that she's got new glasses, she can see what she's smelling!" He tipped his head back and howled with laughter.

The other boys joined right in. "Ha! Ha! Ha!"

"Say, Rachel," Brian hollered, "how's it feel to have four eyes? Do those glasses make you see double?"

Rachel covered her ears to block out their teasing and ran as fast as she could. She didn't want to swing now, so she headed for the schoolhouse.

"Four eyes!"

"Snake eyes!"

"Little bensel!"

The boys scampered past Rachel and raced up the schoolhouse stairs, laughing all the way.

Audra caught up to Rachel and slipped her arm around Rachel's waist. "You should tell the teacher on them. It's not right the way they tease."

Rachel sniffed and swiped at the tears running down her cheeks. "If I tell, they'll call me a retschbeddi and tease me even more."

"Maybe I should tell the teacher then," Audra said.

Rachel shook her head. "Please don't. I'll think of some way to deal with this."

On the way to school the following morning, Rachel made a decision. She decided to take off her glasses before she got to school and put them back on before she got home.

She stopped near the schoolhouse driveway, removed her glasses, and put them inside the small case she'd put in her backpack.

Jacob frowned at Rachel. "What are you doing?"

"What's it look like?"

"It looks like you're not planning to wear your glasses today."

She nodded. "That's right."

"Why?"

"Because I don't like being called four eyes, snake eyes, and little bensel."

"Okay, I won't tease you anymore," Jacob said.

"That won't keep Brian and Orlie from teasing." She started walking again. "I've thought it through, and I've decided not to wear my glasses at school."

"But if you're not wearing your glasses, then how will you see?"

Rachel shrugged. "I'll get by. I got by before, and I'll do it again."

"Don't be lecherich, Rachel. You have to wear your glasses."

"No, I don't."

"Jah, you do. Mom and Pap would be very upset if they knew you weren't wearing your glasses."

Rachel grabbed Jacob's arm. "Promise you won't say anything?"

He shook his head. "I can't promise that. It would be wrong to lie, and you know it."

"I'm not saying you should lie. Just don't tell them I'm not wearing my glasses."

Jacob folded his arms and tapped his foot. "Hmm. . . I don't know, Rachel."

"If you keep quiet, I'll do one of your chores for a whole week."

His eyebrows shot up. "Really?"

She nodded. "Just name a chore—any chore at all, and I'll do it."

"Okay. You can feed and water Buddy."

Rachel wrinkled her nose. "You know what will happen if I go anywhere near that mangy dog of yours."

"Okay, forget I mentioned it. I'll just tell Mom and Pap you put your glasses in your backpack and didn't wear them at school today."

"If you do that you'll be a retschbeddi."

He shrugged. "So, I'll be a tattletale. At least I'll be telling something they should know."

Rachel rubbed her chin as she thought. If she continued to wear her glasses at school, Orlie and Brian would make fun of her. If she didn't wear them and Jacob told Mom and Pap, she'd be in big trouble.

"Oh, all right," she finally agreed. "I'll feed and water Buddy for one week."

As Rachel sat behind her school desk that morning, her stomach knotted. Not only had she promised to feed and water Jacob's flea-bitten mutt, but now that she wasn't wearing her glasses, she couldn't see the writing on the blackboard or read her schoolbooks well.

"*Psst. . .*Audra," Rachel whispered as she leaned across the aisle. "What do the words on the blackboard say?"

"You'd know what they said if you were wearing your glasses." Audra wrinkled her nose. "Why aren't you wearing them?"

Rachel started to respond, but Elizabeth stepped up to her desk. "What's all the talking about, Rachel?"

"She was asking me what's written on the blackboard," Audra said.

Elizabeth looked at Rachel curiously. "Why aren't you wearing your glasses?"

Rachel bit her lip as she tried to think of how to answer her teacher's question.

Elizabeth tapped her foot. "I'm waiting, Rachel."

"Well, I—uh—don't have my glasses with me today."

"Why not?"

Rachel swallowed. She knew it was wrong to lie, but was afraid to tell the truth. If she told Elizabeth that her glasses were in her backpack, Elizabeth would ask why. Then she'd have to tattle on the boys who had made fun of her.

Elizabeth touched Rachel's shoulder. "Why didn't you bring your glasses with you today?"

"I—uh—forgot them."

"I see. Well, since you're having a problem seeing the blackboard, I'm going to move your desk close to the front of the room like I did before you got glasses." Elizabeth pushed Rachel's desk to the front row.

Rachel followed with her head down. She heard a few snickers from some of the boys and ground her teeth. If she had to sit up front every day, all the scholars would watch her. On the other hand, if she admitted that she'd lied about leaving her glasses at home, she'd be in trouble with Elizabeth and be embarrassed in front of the class.

Rachel bit the end of a fingernail. *Why do I always have so much trouble?*

Chapter 9

Plenty of Trouble

When Rachel headed to school the next day, she stopped near the schoolhouse driveway, took off her glasses, and put them in her backpack.

"I forgot to ask. . .how'd it go when you fed Buddy last night?" Jacob asked.

"It went fine. He was so hungry he headed straight for his food." Rachel smiled. "I was surprised he didn't lick me, not even once."

"That's good, I guess." Jacob leaned close to Rachel. "So how long do you plan to keep taking your glasses off before you get to school?"

She shrugged.

"You're not gonna do well with your schoolwork if you can't see."

"I can see. Some things are blurry, that's all."

"Jah, well, Mom and Pap paid good money for those glasses, and you should be wearing them to school."

Rachel yanked the zipper closed on her backpack. "I might wear them to school if I knew certain people wouldn't say mean things!"

"Want me to have a talk with Orlie and Brian?"

She shook her head. "They'd probably think I was a retschbeddi who had to ask her older bruder to speak for her."

"Then speak to them yourself. Wouldn't that be better than not being able to see clearly and lying about forgetting to bring your glasses to school?"

Rachel thought about that a few seconds. She didn't feel good about lying, but she didn't feel good about being made fun of, either. Would it help if she tried talking to Orlie and Brian? If she could get them to stop teasing, she'd be able to wear her glasses at school again.

She glanced across the playground and saw Orlie near the swings, talking to Brian. *Maybe I will try talking to them*, she decided. "I'll be right back," she said to Jacob.

"Where are you going?" he asked.

"I'm going to have a little talk with Orlie and Brian."

"Want me to come with you?"

"No thanks. I think I should do this on my own."

"Okay; suit yourself."

Rachel hurried off. By the time she got to the

swings, only Orlie was there. Brian was on the teeter-totter with Audra.

"Hey, Rachel," Orlie said, "I see you're not wearing your other set of eyes today. You sure look funny in those glasses."

Rachel shook her finger. "You should be ashamed of yourself for saying such mean things to me. I used to think you were my friend, but not anymore."

A smile flickered across Orlie's face. "Aw, come on, Rachel, don't take everything so personally." He brushed past her as the school bell rang. "See you inside, four eyes."

Rachel grimaced. She'd probably never be able to wear her glasses to school without being teased. She stomped toward the schoolhouse. *I'll probably be feeding and watering Jacob's dog until I graduate from school!*

"Where are your glasses?" Elizabeth asked when Rachel sat at her desk.

"I—I forgot them again." Each lie Rachel told seemed to cause another lie, and even though she knew it was wrong, she couldn't seem to stop.

"You'll have to sit close to the blackboard then," Elizabeth said. "And if you keep forgetting your glasses, I'll have to send a note home to your parents asking that they remind you to wear them to school."

Rachel gulped. She couldn't let that happen. She'd

have to think of something to keep Mom and Pap from finding out she hadn't worn her glasses to school for two days, and she'd have to think of it soon!

"Good morning, boys and girls," Elizabeth said, after she'd tapped the bell on her desk."

"Good morning, Elizabeth," the scholars replied.

Elizabeth opened her Bible and read a verse of scripture, but Rachel didn't even hear the words. All she could think about was how miserable she felt, and wondered what to do about her glasses.

When it was time to do her schoolwork, Rachel had to lean close to her book to read. Even then, some words were blurry, and her eyes watered from staring so hard. She was tempted to turn around and ask Phoebe to tell her what some of the words were, but if she did that, and Elizabeth saw her, she'd be in trouble again.

Hee-hee. Rachel heard snickering to her right, and she glanced that way. Brian grinned at her as he made circles with his fingers, and then held them in front of his eyes like he was wearing glasses.

Rachel swallowed hard and looked away. She was going to cry if she wasn't careful.

Brian snickered again, but Rachel refused to look at him.

On the way home from school that day, Rachel waited

until they were a safe distance from the schoolhouse. Then she opened her backpack, took out her glasses, and put them on her face. It was a relief to be able to see things clearly again. She wished she felt free to wear her glasses at school.

"What are you going to do when we get home?" Jacob asked.

She shrugged. "I don't know."

"Don't forget about feeding and watering Buddy."

"I won't forget." She groaned. "But I wish I could."

Jacob poked her arm. "Aw, you'll get used to it after a while. You might even think it's kind of fun."

Rachel glared at him. "I'll never get used to that mutt's smelly breath or his slimy tongue slurping my face. He's nothing but a big hairy mutt!"

Jacob chuckled and sprinted for home.

When Rachel entered their yard, she spotted Grandpa in the garden. He called her over to him. "Let's go see what Grandpa wants," Rachel said when she caught up to Jacob.

"You go ahead," he said. "I'm going to change into my work clothes and help Pap and Henry in the fields."

"Okay. See you at supper." Rachel sprinted across the yard to the garden.

"How was your day, Rachel?" Grandpa asked. A smudge of dirt decorated his cheek, and if Rachel hadn't felt so sad she might have laughed.

"My day was all right."

"Just all right?"

She nodded slowly.

"Well, how would you like to help me plant some seeds?"

"Are they vegetable seeds or flower seeds?"

"They're flower seeds, and when the flowers get big enough I hope to sell some of them in my green-house." Grandpa's blue eyes twinkled like fireflies on a hot summer evening, and his bushy gray eyebrows jiggled. "Even though the building's not up yet, I need to prepare and stock up on things."

"I guess that's a good idea," Rachel said.

"So, would you like to help me?"

"Jah, okay. I'll plant some seeds."

"You should run into the house and change out of your school clothes first," Grandpa said.

She nodded. "I'll do that right now."

Rachel scurried into the house. She stopped in the kitchen long enough to tell Mom hello, then rushed upstairs to change out of her school dress. When she came down a few minutes later she saw a plate of pea-nut butter cookies on the table.

"Jacob had a few cookies before he went out to the fields," Mom said. "Would you like to sit at the table and have something to eat?"

She shook her head. "I don't have time. I'm going to help Grandpa plant some flower seeds."

"Why don't you take a few cookies for you and Grandpa?" Mom suggested.

"That's a good idea. Grandpa might be hungry." Rachel plucked four cookies off the plate, wrapped them in a napkin, and scooted out the door. Her bare feet tingled as she skipped across the lawn. Maybe this wasn't such a bad day after all.

"Are you hungry? Mom sent some cookies for us," Rachel said when she joined Grandpa in the garden.

"That sounds good. I've been working hard, and the hurrier I go the behinder I seem to get. Maybe a little break and some tasty cookies will fuel my fire."

Rachel smiled. Grandpa Schrock always said such funny things. She remembered him saying that he liked to tell one joke every day.

Rachel opened the napkin, gave Grandpa two cookies, and ate the other two. "If you're tired, why don't you sit on the porch and rest?" she suggested.

"That's not a bad idea," he said. "After I show you what to do I might sit a few minutes and rest my back."

"Is your back hurting today?"

"Not really, but it gets a little stiff if I try to do too much."

"Then you'd better sit." Rachel patted Grandpa's

hand. "Once you show me what to do, I'm sure I can manage."

"I'm sure you can, too." Grandpa smiled. "Are you getting used to your glasses, Rachel?"

"Uh—jah, I guess so."

"I'll bet you're doing better in school now that you can see things more clearly."

Rachel swallowed. *What would Grandpa think if he knew I've been taking my glasses off at school? He'd probably lecture me and tell Mom and Pap.*

"It'll sure be exciting when we have a greenhouse," Rachel said.

Grandpa nodded. "I love working with flowers. Every day in my new greenhouse will be exciting for me."

"I hope I'll be able to help out."

"When you're not doing other things, I'd appreciate the help." He handed her a packet of seeds. "Are you ready to plant?"

"Jah, sure."

Grandpa explained which seeds Rachel should plant and where he wanted them planted. "I'll give you one packet now, and when you finish that, if you still want to help, you can have more."

"Okay, Grandpa."

"Guess I'll head to the porch now and stretch out on a lawn chair for a little while." Grandpa turned to go but stubbed his bare toe on a rock and yelped.

"Are you okay?" Rachel asked, rushing forward.

"It smarts a bit, but I'll be all right." A smile spread across Grandpa's face. "Do you know what a big toe is best used for?" he asked.

She shook her head.

"It's a way to locate sharp objects in the dark," he said with a deep chuckle. "I've always been good at stubbing my toe whenever I get out of bed at night."

Rachel snickered. What a fun-loving grandpa she had. She wished she could feel this happy all the time.

Grandpa patted the top of Rachel's head. "I'm off to rest now. Let me know when you need more seeds."

"Okay."

When Grandpa walked away, Rachel took the tip of her shovel and made a long, shallow rut in the dirt. Then she opened the packet of sunflower seeds and was about to drop some into the dirt, when—*floop!*— Cuddles leaped into the air and hit her hand, scattering seeds everywhere.

"Ach, Cuddles, now look what you've done! I'll never get all these seeds picked up!" Rachel glanced at the house to see if Grandpa had seen what happened, but he didn't move. She figured he'd fallen asleep.

Ribet! Ribet! Rachel spotted a frog leaping through the garden. Since she couldn't do much with the seeds Grandpa had given her, she thought it might be fun to try and catch the frog.

She crawled slowly along, and when the frog stopped beneath one of the rhubarb plants, Rachel reached out her hand.

Meow! Cuddles leaped through the air and pounced in the dirt near the frog.

The frog jumped. *Ribet! Ribet!*

Cuddles jumped. *Meow! Meow!*

Back and forth across the garden they dashed, kicking up the dirt and scattering the sunflower seeds Rachel had spilled. She didn't know whether to laugh or cry.

Ribet! Ribet! The frog hopped out of the garden and leaped away.

Cuddles chased it.

Rachel grunted and brushed the dirt from her dress. Then she hurried across the lawn. When she stepped onto the porch she saw that Grandpa's eyes were closed. She didn't know whether she should wake him or not.

Suddenly, Grandpa's eyes snapped open. "What's wrong, Rachel?" he asked. "You're clenching your teeth so hard your cheeks are twitching."

"I had some problems with the seeds," she said.

He yawned and stretched his arms over his head. "What kind of problems?"

"Cuddles was fooling around in the garden and landed on my hand." Rachel frowned. "Then she chased after a frog, and now the seeds are scattered everywhere."

Grandpa reached into his pocket and took out another packet of seeds. "I guess we'll have to start all over again."

"What about the scattered seeds?"

Grandpa squeezed Rachel's shoulder. "Some of the seeds will make a nice meal for the birds that come into our yard, and the rest will probably come up wherever they choose."

Rachel smiled as she followed Grandpa to the garden. She was glad she had such a nice grandfather. He hadn't even yelled or given her a lecture for spilling the seeds.

After Rachel finished helping Grandpa plant two rows of seeds, she went to do her most dreaded chore— feeding and watering Jacob's smelly mutt.

She found the dog food in the barn and scooped some into an empty coffee can. When she got to the dog run, she set the can of food on the ground and struggled to open the squeaky, stubborn gate.

I wish Pap would oil this, Rachel thought. *But if I ask him about it, he'll probably want to know what I was doing in Buddy's dog run. Then I'll have to explain that I was giving food and water to Buddy, and Pap will ask why.* Rachel gritted her teeth. *No, it's best not to say anything about the stubborn gate. After my week of caring for Buddy is over, feeding and watering that unruly hund will be Jacob's worry.*

With another push on the gate, Rachel entered the dog run. She was about to pour food into Buddy's dish when he bounded up to her, wagging his tail. *Woof! Woof! Slurp! Slurp!* He licked her face with his long, pink tongue.

"Get down, you hairy beast!" Rachel pushed Buddy with her knee.

Woof! Woof! Buddy swiped his tongue across her arm.

"Leave me alone! It's time for your supper!" Rachel poured the food into his dish and quickly stepped aside.

Buddy stuck his nose in the dish. *Chomp! Chomp! Chomp!*

Rachel hurried out of the dog run and raced across the yard to get the hose. When she returned to fill Buddy's water dish, he jumped up and knocked the hose out of her hands. A stream of water shot straight up and squirted Rachel's face!

"Now look what you've done, you—you dumm hund!" Rachel sputtered. "Thanks to you, my face is wet!"

Woof! Woof! Buddy darted out of the dog run and tore across the yard.

Rachel chased him. "Come back here, you beast!"

"What's Buddy doing out of his dog run?" Jacob

asked as he came around the side of the barn.

"He got out after he knocked the hose out of my hand." Rachel sniffed. "Thanks to that mutt, my face is wet!"

"Don't cry, Rachel," Jacob said with a grin. "You're already wet enough."

She grunted. "You'd better teach that hund some manners or I'm not going to feed and water him anymore!"

"If you back out of our agreement I'll tell Mom and Pap that you haven't worn your glasses at school for two days," Jacob threatened.

"You wouldn't."

"Jah, I would."

Rachel squeezed her hands into a ball. "You do and I'll tell that you teased me about my glasses, even after you said you wouldn't."

Jacob shrugged. "Go ahead. I'll bet you'll be in a lot more trouble for not wearing your glasses at school than I will for teasing you."

Rachel sighed. "All right, you win." She started for the house, but turned back around. "What are you doing here anyway, Jacob? I thought you were supposed to be out in the field helping Pap and Henry."

"I was, but Pap needed something from the barn. I'll put Buddy back in his pen first, though."

"Good luck with that." Rachel handed Jacob the

empty coffee can and hurried away.

As she stepped onto the porch, the steps creaked beneath her feet; then she heard a bird whistling joyously from a nearby tree. Rachel tilted her head to get a good look at the bird. "At least somebody's happy today," she muttered.

She opened the door, and was greeted with a wonderful aroma coming from the kitchen.

"What are you cooking?" Rachel asked Mom.

Mom turned from the stove and smiled. "Come take a look."

Rachel peered into the kettle sitting on the stove. Chunks of vegetables, slivers of meat, and floating spices made her mouth water. She loved Mom's tasty stews. "Mmm. . .I can't wait for supper."

Mom turned down the stove and shuffled across the room. "Your hair and face are wet, Rachel," she said, lowering herself into a chair. "What did you do, take a drink from the hose?"

Rachel's thoughts tumbled around in her head like a windmill going full speed, as she searched for the right words. "I—uh—got shot in the face with the hose when I was giving Jacob's dog some water."

Mom raised her eyebrows. "Caring for Buddy is supposed to be Jacob's job. Why were you doing it?"

Rachel shifted from one foot to the other. "I—uh—was doing Jacob a favor." The lie stuck in her throat like a glob of gooey peanut butter, only it didn't taste good.

Mom tapped her fingers on the edge of the table. "Did Jacob do a favor for you?"

Rachel shook her head.

"So you just gave Buddy some water to be nice?"

"Uh—jah."

Mom smiled. "That was kind of you. It shows that you're maturing."

Rachel swallowed so hard she nearly choked. "I'm going to the bathroom to wash my hands. When I come back, I'll set the table."

"Danki, Rachel. Take your time."

With the lie she'd told Mom still burning in her throat, Rachel dashed from the room.

Chapter 10

Vanished

When Rachel fed and watered Buddy the next day, things went much better. He licked her hand when she poured food in his dish, but then he ate and left her alone.

"Good dog," Rachel said. She hurried out of the dog run and closed the gate.

Rachel raced back to the barn and put the empty can in the bag of dog food. She'd just turned around when she heard a faint *meow!* Cuddles was curled up on a bale of hay, licking her paws.

Rachel sat on the hay and placed the cat in her lap. "Did you have a hard day today, Cuddles?"

Cuddles nuzzled Rachel's hand with her little pink nose.

"My day wasn't easy, either," Rachel said. "I lied to my teacher and said I forgot to wear my glasses again."

Purrr. . .Purrr. Cuddles kneaded her paws against Rachel's chest.

"Yesterday, Elizabeth said if I forgot my glasses again she would give me a note to take home." Rachel leaned against the wall behind her. "But I think Elizabeth forgot about the note because she never mentioned it again. She has been making me sit near the front of the room, though."

Cuddles lifted her head and opened one eye. *Meow!*

Rachel stroked the cat's ear and closed her eyes. *What can I do about the problem with my glasses?* she wondered. *If I lost my glasses I wouldn't have to wear them at all, and I wouldn't have to keep telling Elizabeth I left them at home.*

Rachel placed Cuddles on the bale of hay. She glanced around the barn, wondering where she might safely put her glasses. She spotted a small box on a shelf near the door and went to look at it.

The box was empty, so she took off her glasses and placed them inside. Then she slipped the box under her arm and climbed the ladder to the hayloft.

Let's see. . .where's a good place to hide this box?

Rachel noticed several bales of hay stacked against the wall, so she wedged the box between them.

Screech. It sounded like someone had come into the barn. "Who's there?" Rachel called.

No response.

She listened. "Jacob, is that you?"

No answer—just a snorting sound coming from the

stall where Pap kept his buggy horse.

Rachel scurried down the ladder and raced out of the barn.

When Rachel entered the kitchen, she found Mom in front of the sink, humming as she peeled potatoes. "Is it time to start supper?" Rachel asked.

"I've started the potatoes, so you can set the table." Mom turned from the sink. "Ach, Rachel, why aren't you wearing your glasses?"

"Well, I—uh—don't know where they are." Another lie slid off Rachel's tongue as easily as she and Jacob slid down the hay chute in their barn. One lie seemed to lead to another. . .and another. . .and another.

Mom's eyebrows shot up. "You lost your glasses?"

Rachel nodded and stared at the floor.

"You were wearing them when you got home from school, right?"

"Jah."

"Where'd you put them?"

"I—I don't know."

"Think about it, Rachel. Did you take them off to wash your face after school?"

Rachel shook her head. "I haven't washed my face since this morning."

"Where have you been since you got home? Let's retrace your steps."

Rachel's heart pounded. She hated lying to Mom, but if she told the truth now, she'd be in big trouble— and she'd be forced to wear her glasses at school.

"Where have you been?" Mom asked again.

"I—uh—took a walk to the garden, and then I went to—" Rachel halted her words. She'd almost told Mom that she'd fed and watered Buddy again. If she let that slip, Mom would ask why she was doing Jacob's chore for the second day in a row, and she might get suspicious.

Mom started for the door. "Let's go outside and look for them. Maybe they fell off your face when you were in the garden. Or they could be somewhere on the lawn."

With shoulders slumped, Rachel followed Mom out the door.

When they reached the garden, Mom walked between the rows while Rachel stood to one side.

"What are you looking for, Miriam?" Grandpa asked when he joined them in the garden.

"Rachel's glasses," Mom said. "They seem to have vanished."

"Is that so?" Grandpa looked over at Rachel. "You were wearing your glasses when you came home from school; isn't that right?"

"Jah."

"Where have you been since you got here?" he asked.

Rachel kicked at a clump of grass. "I'm—uh—not sure."

"She said she came out here to the garden, but I don't see her glasses anywhere," Mom said.

Grandpa scratched his bearded cheek. "Did you go to your room to change your clothes after school?"

Rachel nodded.

"Maybe you left your glasses there."

"I don't think so." Every lie Rachel told burned in her throat like a lump of hot coal. She figured the best thing to do was go out to the barn, get her glasses, and say that she'd found them. "I—uh—think I know where I left them," she mumbled.

"Where would that be?" asked Mom.

"In the barn. I went there to pet Cuddles," Rachel said. "I'll go and see."

"I was going to walk out to the fields to see if your daed's done for the day," Grandpa said. "Maybe I should go to the barn and help you look for your glasses instead."

Rachel shook her head. "That's okay. I'm sure I can find them."

"All right then. I'm off to the fields." Grandpa headed in that direction.

"I'm going back in the house to finish peeling potatoes," Mom said. "If you don't find your glasses in the barn, let me know and we'll get your daed and *brieder* [brothers] to help us look as soon as they come in from the fields."

"Okay." Rachel raced into the barn, scampered up the ladder to the hayloft, and dropped to her knees in front of the bales of hay. She slipped her hands into the place where she'd hidden the box and gasped. It was gone!

She searched again, looking between every bale of hay. A chill rippled through her body. No box! No glasses! She knew she had no choice but to go back to the house and tell Mom that she'd hidden her glasses in the hayloft and now they were gone. A sudden thought shook her all the way to her toes. Someone must have found the box and taken it! But who?

With tears burning her eyes and legs trembling like a newborn colt, Rachel climbed down the ladder. She'd just stepped out of the barn when she spotted her schoolteacher's horse and buggy at the hitching rail.

It's almost suppertime. I wonder what Elizabeth's doing here?

Rachel hurried into the house and found Elizabeth in the kitchen, talking to Mom.

Mom frowned at Rachel. "Elizabeth has given me distressing news. She said you haven't worn your glasses at school for the last few days."

Thump! Thumpety! Thump! Thump! Rachel's heart hammered as she stared at the floor.

"Is it true, Rachel?" Mom asked.

"Jah."

"But you were wearing your glasses before you left for school every day this week. You never mentioned losing them until this afternoon."

Rachel shifted from one foot to the other as tears welled in her eyes. The lies she'd told had only made things worse. She wished she could take them all back.

"Rachel, answer me, please."

"I—I took off my glasses before I got to school, and I—I put them in my backpack," Rachel said in a quavering voice.

"But you told me you'd forgotten your glasses at home," Elizabeth said.

"I—I'm sorry I lied." *Sniff! Sniff!* Rachel wiped the tears rolling down her cheeks.

"I don't understand. Why did you lie about leaving your glasses at home?" Mom asked.

"Some of the boys at school made fun of my glasses, and I—I felt ugly wearing them." Rachel's voice broke on a sob. "So I—I decided not to w—wear them at school anymore."

"What?" Mom's mouth fell open, and her glasses slipped to the end of her nose.

"Why didn't you tell me about the teasing?" Elizabeth asked.

"I was afraid they'd call me a retschbeddi and tease me more."

"At times it's necessary to tell on someone, and this was one of those times." Elizabeth placed her hand on Rachel's shoulder. "Your glasses don't make you look ugly, and you shouldn't worry about what others think or say. It's important that you wear your glasses so you can see well enough to do your schoolwork."

"Elizabeth is right," Mom agreed. "You should have told her and us about the teasing, and you shouldn't have lied about losing your glasses."

Rachel nodded. "I know, and I'm truly sorry."

Mom touched the tip of Rachel's nose. "Where are your glasses now? Are they really lost, or did you put them in your backpack again?"

Rachel swallowed around the lump in her throat. "I—I put them in a box I found in the barn, and I hid them in the hayloft."

"Then you'd better get them, schnell," Mom said.

"I went there a few minutes ago," Rachel said tearfully, "but the box was gone." She drew in a shaky breath. "Now my glasses really *have* vanished."

Mom's forehead wrinkled. "You truly don't know where they are?"

Rachel shook her head. "I'm afraid I might never see my glasses again."

Just then the back door opened and Jacob stepped into the kitchen. "What's going on? I saw Elizabeth's horse and buggy outside."

"Your teacher came by to tell me that Rachel hasn't been wearing her glasses at school." Mom stared at Jacob. "Did you know that Rachel had been putting her glasses in her backpack before she got to school?"

Jacob nodded, and his face turned red.

"Why didn't you tell Elizabeth or us what was going on?"

"Well, I—"

Elizabeth cleared her throat. "I think I'd better head for home and let you work things out with your kinner."

"Jah, of course." Mom followed Elizabeth to the door. When she returned to the kitchen she turned to Jacob and said, "I'd like to know why you kept quiet about Rachel not wearing her glasses at school."

"I made him promise not to," Rachel spoke up.

"Did you now?" Mom gave Jacob a curious stare. "What did Rachel promise to do in order for you to keep quiet?"

The color in Jacob's cheeks deepened. "She said she'd feed and water Buddy for a whole week."

Tap! Tap! Tap! Mom's foot thumped against the kitchen floor. "I'm disappointed in both of you." She slowly shook her head. "Now Rachel's glasses are missing, and if they're not found we'll have to buy her a new pair." *Tap! Tap! Tap!* "That's money we don't have to spare right now."

"Rachel's glasses aren't lost," Jacob said. "I know where they are."

Rachel's mouth fell open and she gasped. "You do?"

He nodded. "I was in one of the horse's stalls when you hid your glasses in the hayloft. After you left the barn, I went up there and found the box. I hid it in my room."

"I thought I heard someone in the barn." Rachel glared at Jacob. "Why'd you take my glasses?"

"To teach you a lesson."

"What a mean thing to do, Jacob Yoder!" Rachel's chin trembled. "What were you trying to do—get me in trouble?"

"You're the one who didn't want to wear your glasses."

"That's true, but—"

Mom stepped between them. "No more quarreling! You both did wrong things, and you shall both be punished." She pointed to the stairs. "Jacob, go up to your room and get Rachel's glasses!"

"All right, Mom." Jacob hurried out of the room and sprinted up the stairs.

Mom turned to Rachel. "From now on you are to wear your glasses at school and at home. Is that clear?"

Rachel nodded as tears dribbled down her cheeks. "I will, Mom. Even if the kinner at school tease me, I promise I'll wear my glasses."

Chapter 11

Happy Medicine

"I wish I could have stayed home today," Rachel mumbled as she and Jacob walked to school the next day. She picked up a twig and sent it flying. "And I wish I didn't have to wear glasses!"

Jacob pulled the strings on Rachel's kapp. "*Grummel net um mich rum* [Don't grumble around me]."

Rachel pushed his hand away. "I have good reason to grumble."

"Why?"

"You ought to know, Jacob. I have to wear my glasses to school, and when I get there, I'll have to put up with Orlie and Brian calling me names." Rachel kicked at a pebble. "If that's not bad enough, I have double chores to do for two whole weeks, and I can't go anywhere or do anything fun—all because we lied to Mom and Pap."

Jacob shook his head. "Not *we*, Rachel. It was *you* who lied. All I did was promise not to tell Mom and

Pap you weren't wearing your glasses at school."

Rachel ground her teeth together. "Humph! You forced me to feed and water your dumm hund!"

"I didn't force you to take care of Buddy. You said you'd do it if I kept quiet about the glasses." He poked her arm. "And don't forget, I have double chores, too. I'll be working late in the fields tonight, so I was wondering if you would feed Buddy for me."

"You're kidding, right?"

He shook his head.

"After all that mutt did to me the other day, you expect me to go back in his pen?" Rachel shook her head so hard the ties on her kapp flipped up in her face.

"No, I'm never feeding your hund again!"

He grunted. "Fine then! Be that way, little bensel!"

Rachel kicked another rock so hard it hurt her toe. She was tired of Jacob calling her a silly child, and she was worried about how things would go today at school!

When Rachel entered the schoolyard, she spotted Orlie on the porch. She wished he would move. She didn't want to be around him.

Rachel waited near the swings until the school bell rang. When Orlie went inside, she hurried up the stairs and into the schoolhouse. She halted when she saw Orlie standing near the shelf where their lunch pails were kept.

"I see you remembered to wear your glasses," Orlie said.

She brushed past him and put her lunch pail on the shelf.

Orlie followed. "Aren't you talking to me? Did you lose your voice on the way to school? Should we send out a search party to look for it?"

Rachel ground her teeth together, determined to ignore him.

"What's the matter, four eyes? Why are you wearing such a big old frown?"

"Leave me alone. I have nothing to say to you, Orlie Troyer!" Rachel whirled around and hurried to her desk.

Ding! Ding! Ding! Elizabeth rang the bell on her desk. "Good morning, boys and girls."

"Good morning, Elizabeth," Rachel said with the others in her class.

Elizabeth opened her Bible. "I'll be reading from Ephesians 4:32: 'Be kind and compassionate to one another, forgiving each other, just as in Christ God forgave you.'"

Elizabeth closed the Bible and looked at the class. "Before we recite the Lord's Prayer, there's something I'd like to say." She leaned forward with her elbows on the desk. "Poking fun at someone and making rude remarks is wrong. I won't tolerate anyone in this class making fun of another person for any reason at all. Do you understand?"

All heads bobbed up and down, and Rachel breathed a sigh of relief. She hoped none of the scholars would say mean things to her anymore.

During recess that afternoon, Rachel sat on a swing while most of the others played baseball.

"Hey, Rachel, aren't you going join us?" Jacob called from the ball field.

Rachel shook her head. She was afraid if she played ball, her glasses might fall off. She remembered Mom saying she could make a special strap to hold the glasses in place, but Rachel had talked Mom out of it.

Orlie walked by Rachel and snickered.

"What's so funny?" she asked.

He held up four fingers and pointed to his eyes.

Rachel turned her head and looked the other way. Should she say something to their teacher or ignore Orlie's teasing?

She pumped her legs faster. *I'll ignore him. Jah, that would be the best thing to do.*

Rachel stayed on the swing until the ball game was over. When she headed to the schoolhouse, Brian sauntered up to her and made circles with his fingers and placed them around his eyes like he was looking through a pair of glasses.

Rachel looked away. She would ignore him just as she'd done with Orlie.

*Hisss. . .Hisss. . .*Brian smirked at Rachel but didn't say a word. He headed for the schoolhouse, hissing like a snake all the way.

Audra grabbed her brother's arm. "Stop teasing Rachel! If you don't, I'm going to tell the teacher!"

"If you do, I'll tell Mom and Dad you're a retschbeddi."

"I don't care if you do tell them I'm a tattletale. You either stop teasing Rachel, or I'm going to tell Elizabeth!"

"Whatever," Brian mumbled as he walked away.

Audra hugged Rachel. "I'm sorry my bruder is such a *pescht* [pest]."

Rachel swallowed around the lump in her throat and struggled not to cry. "My life's been miserable ever since I got glasses. I wish I could see better without them."

"Try not to be so sad. If you ignore the boys, they'll get tired of teasing you." Audra patted Rachel's back. "Things will get better soon, you'll see."

Rachel kicked at a clump of grass. "I wish I *could* see."

Audra gave Rachel a strange look.

"I wish I could see without my glasses."

"Just be glad someone invented glasses. Millions of people in the world wouldn't be able to see well if it weren't for their glasses."

"I guess you're right," Rachel said. "Even so, I wish I wasn't one of the millions who need glasses."

When Rachel got home from school, Mom had a list of chores waiting for her. One of them was taking the dry towels off the line.

"I wish I didn't have so many chores all the time," Rachel grumbled as she lugged the wicker basket to the clothesline.

Plunk! Plunk! Plunk! She pulled the pins from the towels and dropped everything into the basket.

Rachel glanced across the yard and saw Cuddles running out of the barn. Tears trickled down Rachel's cheeks, and she reached up to wipe them away. *I wish I could play with Cuddles instead of doing chores. I wish I wasn't me.*

Rachel picked up the basket and turned toward the house. She'd only taken a few steps, when—*Honk! Honk!*—their mean old goose charged across the lawn. Rachel remembered the last time the goose had pecked the backs of her legs. She didn't want that to happen again, so she ran for all she was worth!

By the time Rachel reached the back porch, she was huffing and puffing so much she could barely catch her breath.

Thump! Thump! Thump! She hurried up the steps

and turned to see if the goose had followed. *Honk! Honk!* The goose flapped her wings, stuck out her long neck, and pecked at the porch.

Rachel set the basket down and fluttered her hands. "Shoo! Shoo! Go away you ornery goose!"

Clip-clop! Clip-clop! A horse and buggy rolled into the yard. The horse whinnied and pawed the ground. The goose honked and waddled away.

"Good riddance," Rachel muttered.

"Hello, Rachel!" Esther called as she climbed down from the buggy. "Is Mom home?"

Rachel nodded. "She's in the house writing a letter to Aunt Irma."

Esther smiled as she stepped onto the porch. "I need to do some letter writing of my own." She patted her stomach. "But with the boppli coming this fall, I've been busy sewing baby clothes and painting the baby's room. So I haven't had the time to write any letters."

"Speaking of letters. . .I got one from Mary a few weeks ago."

"That's nice. What did Mary say?"

"She said they'd gone to the Fun Spot amusement park." Rachel groaned. "I asked Pap if he'd take us to Hershey Park sometime, but he said he was too busy, and that Mom wasn't up to such an outing right now."

"I don't expect she would be." Esther patted the top of Rachel's head. "Maybe after our baby brother or sister is born, Pap will take the whole family to Hershey Park."

Rachel folded her arms and frowned. "I doubt it. Once the boppli comes, Pap will probably think of some other reason we can't go."

Esther put her thumb under Rachel's chin and tipped her head up so Rachel was looking right at her. "Now what's that sour expression all about? You look like you've been sucking on a bunch of bitter grapes."

Rachel pointed to her glasses. "Ever since I got these, I've had nothing but trouble!"

"What kind of trouble?"

"Boys at school say mean things to me." Rachel sniffed. "Orlie called me 'four eyes,' and Brian said my glasses make me look like a snake."

Esther hugged Rachel. "I'm sure the boys were only teasing. That's what most boys like to do, you know." She laughed, but Rachel didn't think it was one bit funny.

She nudged the wicker basket with her toe and grunted. "I hid my glasses and lied about it to Mom. Now I've got double chores to do for two whole weeks!"

"I'm sorry to hear you lied, Rachel." Esther frowned. "I hope you realize that it was the wrong thing to do."

Rachel nodded as a familiar lump lodged in her throat.

"Mom and Pap love you very much, but it's their job as good parents to punish their children when they do something wrong, especially when it goes against God's teachings."

Rachel nodded again, as tears flooded her eyes.

Esther patted Rachel's shoulder. "Now put on a happy face, do what's right, and things are bound to get better."

Rachel stared at the basket of towels. "I don't see how I can put on a happy face when I have so many chores."

"You have many reasons to smile. I have a bookmark at home that lists 101 reasons to smile." Esther chuckled. "Of course, I can't remember all of them, but here are a few: last day of school, a warm summer day, a beautiful sunset, fresh-cut flowers, and an unexpected hug." She pulled Rachel to her side and hugged her again. "Maybe what you need is a good dose of happy medicine."

Rachel tilted her head. "Happy medicine?"

"Come with me and I'll show you." Esther took Rachel's hand and led her down the steps. When she came to a patch of dirt, she squatted down and picked up a twig. Then she drew a heart in the dirt, and added a smiley face. "Make up your mind to be happy, learn to find pleasure in simple things, and whenever you're feeling sad and grumpy, quote this verse from

Proverbs 17:22: " 'A cheerful heart is good medicine, but a crushed spirit dries up the bones.' "

Rachel nodded. "I see what you mean. I'll do my best to have a cheerful heart and put on a happy face."

Chapter 12

A Day of Surprises

Rachel couldn't believe today was the last day of school, but here she was, walking to school carrying Cuddles in a cat carrier.

She glanced at Buddy, plodding along on his leash beside Jacob, grunting and kicking up dust with his big furry paws. *What a goofy dog,* she thought.

Elizabeth had told the scholars they could bring their pets today. Since Rachel knew some dogs might not get along well with her cat, she'd put Cuddles in the carrier to protect her. She would only take the cat out of the carrier if someone wanted to pet or hold her.

"I hope you're planning to keep Buddy tied up," Rachel said, looking at Jacob. "If you don't, he'll probably jump up and lick everyone's face."

Jacob shook his head. "I don't think so. My hund saves all his kisses for you."

"Very funny!"

Jacob snickered. "Come on, Rachel; don't be so

grouchy. You know you like Buddy. He's a good dog."

She shrugged. "He's okay, and I'm glad he and Cuddles have become friends. I just wish he didn't jump up and lick my face all the time."

"Buddy wouldn't do it if he didn't think you were his friend."

Woof! Woof! Buddy wagged his tail and looked at Rachel with big brown eyes.

She patted his head. "I do like you, Buddy. I just don't like your—"

Slurp! Slurp! Buddy licked Rachel's hand with his sloppy pink tongue.

Rachel pulled her hand back. "See what I get for trying to be nice?"

Jacob slapped his knee and chuckled.

Rachel gritted her teeth. She didn't think Buddy's slimy wet kisses were the least bit funny!

"Let's play a game of baseball," Orlie said during afternoon recess. He smiled at Rachel. "Would you like to be on the same team as me and Jacob?"

Rachel shook her head. "I'd rather not play."

"Why not?"

She pointed to her glasses. "I don't want to lose these. They might fall off my face and get broken."

"Oh, come on, Rachel, I'm sure your glasses won't fall," Orlie said. "I'd like you to be on our team."

"Why don't you take your glasses off and leave them on the picnic table?" Audra suggested. "Can you see well enough to play without them?"

Rachel thought about the last time she'd played ball, before she'd gotten her glasses. She'd had trouble seeing the ball when it was thrown to her, and she'd struck out. "I can see some things without my glasses, but not nearly as well as I can with my glasses on," she said. "You go ahead and play without me."

Audra shook her head. "If you're not going to play, neither am I. I'll sit on the sidelines and watch with you."

Rachel didn't want Audra to sit out of the game because of her, but she didn't want to play ball with her glasses on, either.

Audra remained at Rachel's side.

"Okay, I'll play!" Rachel removed her glasses and placed them on the picnic table. She turned to Orlie and said, "You'd better not complain if I don't play well enough."

He grinned. "I won't complain; I promise."

Rachel took her place in center field. The first person up to bat was Aaron King, and he hit a ball that went right into the catcher's mitt.

"You're out!" shouted Orlie. "Two more outs and our team's up to bat."

The game continued, and even though Rachel couldn't see very well without her glasses, she had fun playing ball. By the time the game was over she'd caught a couple of balls and had even made a homerun. She smiled. Even more surprising than how well she played was that no one had made fun of her for wearing glasses. Maybe the boys had decided to quit teasing and leave her alone.

"Can I hold your cat?" Phoebe asked Rachel.

Rachel nodded. "Jah, sure, but let me get my glasses first." She headed across the playground, but when she got to the picnic table, she halted. Her glasses were gone!

She looked around frantically. They weren't on any of the picnic tables.

"Has anyone seen my glasses?" Rachel shouted.

"Not me," said Orlie.

"Me neither," several others said.

Rachel fiddled with the ties on her kapp, fighting the temptation to bite off a fingernail. "They couldn't have just disappeared," she said. "Someone must have them."

"I'll help you look," Audra offered.

"Danki."

"Maybe someone picked up your glasses and took them into the schoolhouse," Audra said. "Should we go see?"

Rachel nodded.

They were almost to the schoolhouse porch, when

Buddy ambled up to Rachel, wagging his tail. *Woof! Woof!*

Rachel's mouth fell open; she could hardly believe her eyes. Her glasses were perched in the middle of Buddy's long nose!

Brian and Jacob looked at each other and laughed. Rachel figured they must have put the glasses on the dog.

Woof! Woof! Buddy pranced in circles.

Now everyone laughed—even Rachel. She had to admit, Jacob's dog looked pretty funny. Even so, she was worried that her glasses might fall off Buddy's nose and get stepped on, so she plucked them off his big hairy nose.

Woof! Woof! Woof! Buddy slurped Rachel's hand.

"Stop that!" She pulled her hand away and put the glasses on her face.

"See, what did I tell you? Buddy likes you, Rachel." Jacob snickered. "He likes you so much he wanted to borrow your glasses."

Rachel shook her head. "I'll bet you're the one who put my glasses on Buddy. You probably did it to irritate me."

"I only did it to make everyone laugh," Jacob said.

"It was kind of funny," Rachel admitted. "But don't do it again, because I don't want my glasses ruined."

"Ah, Buddy wouldn't hurt your glasses."

"If they'd fallen off his nose, he could have stepped

on them."

"Well, they didn't fall off, so don't get so worked up about it."

"I'm not worked up."

"Jah, you are."

"Am not."

Phoebe nudged Rachel's arm. "What about Cuddles? Can I hold her now?"

"Jah, sure." Rachel hurried to Cuddles' cage and was shocked to find the door hanging wide open. She peeked inside and gasped. Cuddles was gone!

"Who took my cat?" she shrieked. "Someone better not be playing a trick on me!"

"What's all the yelling about?" Elizabeth asked as she came out of the schoolhouse.

"Someone opened the door to Cuddles' carrier and now she's gone!" Rachel's voice shook and she bit her lip to keep from sobbing.

"Did any of you open the door to Rachel's cat carrier?" Elizabeth asked.

Everyone shook their heads.

"Has anyone seen the cat?"

"Not me," said Orlie.

"Me neither," Brian put in. "She probably got out while we were playing ball. I'll bet she's long gone."

Tears sprang to Rachel's eyes as she thought about the last time her cat had disappeared. The day Pap's barn burned down, he said he thought all the animals had gotten out of the barn in time. Rachel was worried Cuddles might have been killed in the fire. She'd been relieved to discover that the cat had gone back to the Millers' place where she'd been born.

But this time it might be different, Rachel thought as she looked around helplessly. *This time Cuddles might have gotten lost for good.* She shivered. *I shouldn't have brought Cuddles to school today. I might never see her again.*

Jacob touched Rachel's arm. "Don't look so sad. It'll be okay."

"Jah, don't be sad," Orlie agreed. "I'll bet Cuddles went home. She'll probably be waiting for you when you get there."

Rachel's heart pounded with sudden hope. "D–do you really think so?"

He nodded.

"I agree with Orlie," said Jacob. "Cuddles is a schmaert cat. I'm sure she'll find her way home."

As Rachel walked home from school with Jacob and Buddy, she glanced at Cuddles' empty cat carrier, and a lump formed in her throat. What if Cuddles never came home? What if Rachel never saw her sweet cat again?

"Here Cuddles," she called. "Come, kitty, kitty."

"I don't know why you're calling her." Jacob shook

his head. "Like Orlie and I said earlier, the cat probably went home."

"What if she didn't? What if—"

"Don't be such a worrier," Jacob said. "As Grandma Yoder always says, 'Worry is nothing more than thinking about something you don't want to happen.'"

Rachel blinked against the tears stinging her eyes. "I don't want anything bad to happen to Cuddles."

"Then quit worrying and pray that she's okay."

Rachel nodded. She'd been so worried and upset over Cuddles' disappearance that she'd forgotten to pray. *Dear God,* she prayed silently, *please keep my cat safe and bring her back to me.*

When Jacob and Rachel entered their yard, Rachel made a dash for the house. Cuddles wasn't on the porch.

Rachel dropped the cat carrier and her backpack on the table by the door and raced into the house. "Is Cuddles here?" she asked when she entered the kitchen and found Mom at the table with a glass of iced tea.

Mom shook her head. "I haven't seen Cuddles since you took her to school this morning."

Thump! Thump! Thump! Rachel's heart beat so hard she thought it might burst open. "Cuddles got out of her carrier and now she's missing!"

"She could be in the barn," Mom said.

"I'll go check." Rachel raced out of the house.

"Are you here, Cuddles?" she called when she entered the barn.

"Here kitty, kitty!" Rachel listened carefully.

Only the soft nicker of the horses in their stalls.

Rachel sank to a bale of hay, letting her head fall forward into her hands. This day couldn't get much worse!

Please, God, she prayed through her sniffling sobs. *Please bring Cuddles home to me.*

That evening as Rachel set the table for supper, she kept thinking about her cat. The other day she'd decided to be more cheerful, but now she just wanted to cry.

Rachel had just placed the last dish on the table when Jacob entered the house with a gloomy look.

"What's wrong?" Mom asked. "You look upset."

Jacob nodded. "I am upset. I let Buddy wander around the yard while I went to the barn to get his food, but when I came back, he was gone." He slowly shook his head. "I called and called, but Buddy didn't come. I even tried blowing the silent whistle I bought to train him, but that didn't work, either." His chin quivered as if he was on the verge of tears. "Now my dog and Rachel's cat are both missing."

"I hope Buddy didn't go out on the road," Mom said. "With all the cars going by this time of night, he might have—" Her voice trailed off as she looked out the window. "Well, well. . .what do you know?"

"What is it?" Rachel asked.

Mom motioned to the window. "You'd better come see this, too, Jacob."

Rachel and Jacob scurried over to the window.

"It's Buddy!" Jacob hollered. "He's carrying Cuddles by the scruff of her neck!"

Rachel dashed out the door. "Cuddles! Are you okay?"

Buddy ambled up the steps and set Cuddles on the porch.

Cuddles looked up at Rachel. *Meow!*

Rachel scooped the cat into her arms. This had sure been a day of surprises! "Oh, Cuddles," she said, nuzzling the cat's head with her nose, "I'm so glad to see you!"

Woof! Woof! Woof! Buddy looked up at Rachel as if to say, "Aren't you happy to see me, too?"

Rachel patted Buddy's head. "I don't know where you found Cuddles, but thank you for rescuing her."

Woof! Woof! Buddy wagged his tail and licked Rachel's hand.

This time Rachel didn't mind being slurped by Jacob's hairy mutt. She gave Buddy's head another pat. "Good dog!"

Jacob and Mom came out on the porch, and Jacob

dropped to his knees. He wrapped his arms around Buddy's neck. *Slurp! Slurp! Slurp!* Buddy licked Jacob's nose, his chin, his cheeks, and even his ears.

"Knock it off, Buddy," Jacob said with a grunt. "That's way too many kisses."

Rachel giggled. At least she wasn't the only one getting Buddy's wet, sloppy kisses.

"I wonder where Buddy found Cuddles," Mom said, reaching out to pet the cat.

Rachel shrugged. "I don't know, and I don't care. I'm just glad she's safe and home where she belongs."

Jacob stood and faced Rachel. "This is the second time my dog has rescued your cat, you know."

Rachel nodded. "Buddy and Cuddles have been friends ever since the day Cuddles fell in the creek and Buddy jumped in after her."

Buddy flopped onto the porch with a grunt. Cuddles leaped from Rachel's arms and curled in front of Buddy. She stuck out her little pink tongue and— *Slurp! Slurp!*—licked the end of Buddy's nose. Then she licked his ears, his head, and even his paws. *Slurp! Slurp! Slurp!* She kept on licking.

"Ha! Ha! Ha!" Rachel laughed and laughed. When she finally quit laughing, she looked up at Mom and smiled. "Esther was right when she said it's important to have a happy heart. Right after supper, I'm going to paint a happy face on one of my rocks to remind me, that even when things don't go my way, to smile and put on a happy face."

Recipe for Grandma Yoder's
Maple Syrup Cookies

1 teaspoon baking soda
1 tablespoon milk
1 egg
½ cup plus 2 tablespoons shortening
1 cup maple syrup
3 cups flour
3 teaspoons baking powder
½ teaspoon salt
1 teaspoon vanilla
1 (8 ounce) package semisweet chocolate chips

Preheat oven to 350°. In a small cup, dissolve baking soda in milk and set aside. Cream egg, shortening, and syrup. Add flour, baking powder, salt, vanilla, and baking soda mixture; blend well. Stir in chocolate chips. Drop by teaspoons onto greased cookie sheet and bake 12-15 minutes.

Other books by Wanda E. Brunstetter

Fiction

Rachel Yoder—Always Trouble Somewhere Series
School's Out!
Back to School
Out of Control
New Beginnings
A Happy Heart
Just Plain Foolishness

Sisters of Holmes County Series

Brides of Webster County Series

Daughters of Lancaster County Series

Brides of Lancaster County Series

Nonfiction

Wanda Brunstetter's Amish Friends Cookbook
The Simple Life

Also available from Barbour Publishing

School's Out!

RACHEL YODER—
Always Trouble Somewhere
Book 1
by Wanda E. Brunstetter
ISBN 978-1-59789-233-9

Back to School

RACHEL YODER—
Always Trouble Somewhere
Book 2
by Wanda E. Brunstetter
ISBN 978-1-59789-234-6

Out of Control

RACHEL YODER—
Always Trouble Somewhere
Book 3
by Wanda E. Brunstetter
ISBN 978-1-59789-897-3

New Beginnings

RACHEL YODER—
Always Trouble Somewhere
Book 4
by Wanda E. Brunstetter
ISBN 978-1-59789-898-0

Just Plain Foolishness

RACHEL YODER—
Always Trouble Somewhere
Book 6
by Wanda E. Brunstetter
ISBN 978-1-60260-135-2